THE
TITAN
HOTEL

Part 1

Sanjay Chunnilalji Rajpurohit

Contents

Chapter 1 – 17+69, 34+42, 04+23 9

Chapter 2 – The Titan Model 36

Chapter 3 – Here We Go! 57

Chapter 4 – The Hunt 77

Chapter 5 – The First Guest.........................106

Chapter 6 – The Plan.........................133

Chapter 7 – Execution and Delivery 154

Chapter 8 – The Snake 183

Chapter 9 – Sherkhan.........................202

Chapter 10 – This is Business 222

Chapter 11 – Light, Camera, Action… 238

Chapter 12 – Khamma Ghanni 250

Location: Tihar Jail

Time: 7 PM

A strong, naked bulb hangs from the ceiling, illuminating a circle, beyond which lies a deep and unsettling darkness. Within the circle of light stands a wooden table and 2 chairs facing each other. A young man occupies one of them. He is dressed in a prisoner's uniform, a faint stubble and jail-cropped hair. The records state he was only 30, but his demeanor and the expression in his eyes make him look much older than his age.

The man at the other side of the table is much older, dressed in a spotless white shirt, his lawyer's coat resting on the handles of the chair- sweating profusely and shifting uncomfortably in his chair. The blades of the ceiling fan move in slow- deliberate circles, barely shifting the air around the room, making it stuffy and insufferable- one would expect better facility from one of the country's sought-after (or notorious) prisons.

It had been a while since Ramanuj had been sitting in this unbearable meeting room, begging his client to speak. He can occasionally hear the faint chatter of the

2 constables waiting outside and the scent of tobacco wafting through the air- but the silence in the room stands heavy.

He tries again… "Section 302, 85, 86, 212, 216 The charges against you are uncountable. Do you have any idea what will happen? You will go straight to the gallows and hang until death.

Come on, speak up, boy! Do you not fear death?"

"I am tired of life, and I don't want to live anymore." The man finally spoke in a defiant voice.

"Well, you still have hope," Ramanuj continues to cajole, ignoring his statement.

"Tell me your story, and I will build a strong case. If we work as a team, I can try and bail you out of this mess. The only thing that I need to know is the truth and the entire story, no secrets, no holding back."

Bindu: "It's a long story."

Ramanuj: "I have all the time in the world. This is your only chance if you tell me your story… Otherwise, if I go to court with no information or a pack of lies, my appeal will be rejected, and you will be gone forever… Do you understand?"

After some time

Bindu: "From where do I start? That fateful day, when I stepped into the city of Jaisalmer. The Golden City, the city of dreams… I was excited, about to start a new life. Little did I know that the beautiful, vibrant city would soon be robbed of its happiness. Tell me, how would I know that the price for my ambition would be so great that it would swallow a whole city in its flames, bringing in death and destruction in its wake?"

A chill ran through Ramanuj's spine; who was this boy, a harmless, young convict or a demon?

Bindu: "Have you heard of Jaswant Kumar? Who doesn't know that scoundrel?" he says suddenly, laughing – a dry, mirthful laughter.

Ramanuj sits back; he can sense the story is coming, and this will determine the course of the most controversial case in his career.

Chapter 1

17+69, 34+42, 04+23

5 years from the present date:

2 cars rolled along Jaisalmer's Munabao Road. Kaishav Jain drove the front one, showing off his skills as a land broker. Following closely was a rented black sedan, steered confidently by Jaswant Kumar. Sitting next to him were his stylish wife, Vaishali Kumar, and their cute 6-year-old son.

The Kumar family looked really good. Vaishali wore beige pants and a neat white linen shirt, highlighting her light skin and petite figure. Jaswant Kumar, strong and fair-skinned, had a fancy salt-and-pepper hairstyle. He wore transparent glasses, a light gray shirt, and darker gray trousers, giving him a wise and experienced look.

In the back seat, their little son, a happy kid in blue shorts and a tee, was busy playing a fun video game on his tablet. The rhythmic sound of the wheels on the road, along with the vast desert unfolding outside, created a cool backdrop.

As they left the city behind, Vaishali stared at the changing scenery. The desert, with its wavy sand and never-ending view.

Vaishali gazed out of the window and questioned, "Is it really necessary to do this?"

Jaswant Kumar replied, "Why not?"

Vaishali continued, expressing her skepticism, "Who in their right mind would invest money here?" She gestured toward the barren landscape outside. "There's nothing but sand all around. I don't think this is a good idea."

Jaswant Kumar countered, "Have you ever seen a city or a village near a gold mine? Oil always comes out from land farthest away from human habitation. I believe this wild land has a lot of hidden value within it. It just needs to be tapped into. It's just waiting to be discovered."

Location: 50 km before Munabao village

Time: 9:30 AM

The cars come to a halt, and both parties alight from the car. Kaishav Jain, a tall man dressed in formal white shirt and well-fitted tan trousers, takes off his designer shades and points a finger at the middle of nothing.

"Look at this huge expanse of untouched land. All this could be yours, he says, spreading his hands. If you don't like this, my friend, you will hardly like anything else. Do you know what reminds me of this? *The Nights of Arabia.*"

"Have you seen the movie, Bhabhi?" Kaishav Jain asks, turning around to face Vaishali.

"No, I don't watch movies," Vaishali answers curtly, squinting her eyes against the sun.

Kaishav Jain continues… "I mean, look at this place, desert all around and plains in between. Hardly any such place has been found anywhere in the world, nor has anyone seen such a paradise, but here we are…"

Jaswant Kumar: "Perfect. Let's finalize this."

"So finally, you are ready to move on this?" Kaishav Jain asks in disbelief.

Jaswant Kumar: "Yes."

"Ah! Only a seasoned jeweler knows the value of diamonds, and today, you have picked a diamond of a deal for yourself; you are going to walk into a storehouse of wealth. Mark my words. The cost is a bit high, but you know every good thing has a price, and I assure you, you will get every penny's worth of investment!"

Jaswant Kumar: "What's the rate?"

"Rs 12 per square foot, which is less because…" Jaswant Kumar cuts him short…"How much is the total area?"

Kaishav Jain: "Around 7 acres."

Jaswant Kumar: "Okay. I'm taking it all."

Kaishav Jain, unable to believe the deal he is going to crack, "What! Are you sure?"

Jaswant Kumar: "Yes, Mr. Jain, absolutely sure."

Kaishav Jain: "Marvelous, let's go to the registration office tomorrow. I'm sure you're saying all this in your senses."

Jaswant Kumar: "Who is the owner of this land? I think we should sit and close the deal with him first."

Kaishav Jain: "This is government land. However, the Rajasthan government has passed a bill in which common citizens can buy government land. I don't see any logic in it, but the government took this step to promote tourism more. That's why if someone wants to buy land, then first, the government will see for what purpose you are buying the land. If your purchase increases tourism, then the government will give that land immediately. The fact that you wish to build a hotel in the area that will consequently affect tourism will make this process much easier. The paperwork can be done immediately. Sit back and leave all the worries on me now."

Jaswant Kumar: "Okay then, we will meet tomorrow."

Kaishav Jain: "Great, once you have all the documents ready, give me a call, and I will come and pick you up."

Location: Government Registration Office, Jaisalmer

Time: 10:00 AM (Next Morning)

Jaswant Kumar and Kaishav Jain are deep in conversation inside the car.

Kaishav Jain: "Did you bring what I had asked for?"

Jaswant Kumar: "Yes, but aren't you coming inside?"

Kaishav Jain: "No, no, I have no work inside. But no need to feel scared it's not as if you are doing any illegal work. Just Relax. An old man is sitting inside, and he will do your verification. If they ask which broker showed you the land, don't take my name. Take someone else name.

That's our policy; we only sell land. We don't go beyond that. And especially in a government office, I don't want my work to be visible to everyone. Best of luck."

Jaswant Kumar is sitting inside the waiting room of the registration office, staring at the wall. The wall seems to have been white-washed recently, yet in some places, the paint has started to peel off, revealing a dusty green shade. There is already a small queue ahead of him; he patiently waits his turn. The lady at the desk guarding the office is 'Bhakti Rajpurohit'- as the nameplate on her desk reads. A fair-skinned, overweight woman of around 33, taking down notes now and then on a ledger-like copy and looking up. Finally, after a fifteen-minute wait that seemed endless, she peeps into the curtained door, gets back to her seat, and calls out,

"Jaswant Kumar, it's your number… you can go in now."

Jaswant Kumar almost leaps to his feet and enters the room.

Chhagan Singh, the government registrar, is waiting behind a pile of files, a balding, overweight man of over 70. He has fair leather-like skin and quick, cunning eyes. He motions Jaswant Kumar to sit and starts examining his documents.

Chhagan Singh: "Your name is Jaswant Prithviraj Kumar, right?"

Jaswant Kumar: "Yes, Sir."

Chhagan Singh: "And you are from Mumbai?"

Jaswant Kumar: "Yes, I came to Jaisalmer only a few days back."

Chhagan Singh: "So, as mentioned in the document, you wish to buy this land to set up a hotel business. Any specific reason? Because of the conditions of the land, its position doesn't seem very business friendly."

Jaswant Kumar: "It is a tourist place, Sir, so I think this can be a great choice of location. People from all over India come to Jaisalmer. After all, I don't see any dearth of opportunities here."

Chhagan Singh: "Kaishav Jain showed this land?"

Jaswant Kumar: "No, who, Kaishav?"

Chhagan Singh: "There is only one broker in the whole of Jaisalmer, Kaishav Jain. Let me guess; he must have asked you not to take his name?"

Jaswant Kumar responds reluctantly, "Yes."

Chhagan Singh: "I do not talk as much or tell things in detail, but you seem to be from a good family; that is why I consider it necessary to tell a story.

Many years ago, a village had become a victim of a plague-like disease. The villagers chose a person who used to kill rats. This person would find a rat hole, put his hand inside, hunt down the rat and crush it with his bare hands. He started enjoying this work so much so that he forgot that not every burrow is a rat hole. Snakes also live in the billows. One day, as he put his long, slender hands inside a hole, a venomous snake bit him.

Now tell me one thing: 17+69, 34+42, 04+23. Is this the exact compass number of that land?"

Jaswant Kumar is a little bewildered by the story the government official just recounted; trying to make a connection between the land and the story, he absent-mindlessly responds, "That's correct."

Chhagan Singh: "Let me tell you that this land has been illegally occupied by a goon named Kalu Singh; he is currently serving a life sentence in jail. Do you know why? He brutally killed 12 people in one go. He is a beast in human disguise. He is a beast who has crossed every limit. You are here; that is why I am telling you. Do you have a family? How many children do you have?"

Jaswant Kumar: "One."

Chhagan Singh: "Had I been in your place, I would have thought a thousand times before doing anything. You can still change your mind before getting into trouble."

Jaswant Kumar storms out of the government office. Kaishav Jain's car is still parked in front of the registration office.

Kaishav Jain: "Work done?"

Jaswant Kumar: "First, tell me, how many brokers are there in Jaisalmer?"

Kaishav Jain contemplates the question for a minute, "Hmmm, I guess it's only me."

Jaswant Kumar: "Then why did you ask me to keep your name out of this?"

Kaishav Jain: "Oh, I didn't really think so hard. Do you know once my father thought of becoming a stand-up comedian? Because he thought laughter was the best medicine, but thinking too hard gave him a heart attack! Hahahaha."

Jaswant Kumar is staring at him.

Jaswant Kumar: "Are you joking? Seriously. Will you please now tell me who this Kalu Singh without any joke is?"

Kaishav Jain: "I anticipated the old man would share that story with you, which is why I preferred to keep my name out of it, just in case he considered letting the matter be. Unfortunately, he didn't, and now I observe he has succeeded in casting doubt upon you…"

Jaswant Kumar: "I don't understand; why did you show me the disputed land?"

Kaishav Jain: "Once the land has been controversial, but not now. Understand the difference. Kalu Singh has been locked in jail for the past 3 years. And his whole life is going to be spent in jail. He tried to get bail many times, but the court did not grant him bail. Why would it? Think, he is accused of murdering 12 people. It is impossible for him to come out of it. When he is not going to come out, then why are you worried? The troublemaker is safely locked up forever."

Jaswant Kumar: "You could have told me all this before."

I didn't tell you because I didn't think it necessary, Kaishav Jain replies. It has been 3 years since the chapter of Kalu Singh is closed. As I said, he is rotting in Jodhpur

Jail. For the time being, he is more concerned about himself than the land. Don't listen to that old man.

Jaswant Kumar goes silent; he is thinking what to do…

Kaishav Jain: "If you want, I can show you more locations; there is no compulsion. If you don't feel right going ahead with this, then don't do it. You know, my grandmother used to say that the work in which the mind gets upset, that sourness remains for the whole life. It is wise not to do that work at all."

"Show me more locations," Jaswant Kumar says, staring straight ahead.

Kaishav Jain: "Why not… I will show you the place just as you want. Excellent views that will remind one of paradise. It's called Ragistani Jannat."

Location: Ramgarh, Jaisalmer

Time: 3:00 PM

Here, look at this glorious place, Kaishav Jain says, spreading his hands in a semi-circle. In the middle of nowhere yet connected by a proper road, the road leads to Tanot Temple, which is very famous around here. No hotel in the vicinity… You will have exclusivity, and all the travelers will come and stop by your hotel.

You can charge whatever you want; people will not question you because what matters here is service, not money. Imagine the demands; this could be a jackpot. Mr Kumar, jackpot."

Jaswant Kumar: "No, I don't like this place."

Kaishav Jain: "Are you sure? I have shown you at least 10 locations, and you like none of them? Now, there is none left to show."

Jaswant Kumar: "You are not getting me. There are countless hotels in this world. I don't want to build just another hotel. Only those things work in the world which are different from the rest, something that the world has never seen or experienced before. Exclusivity and comfort are the 2 things people look for when staying at a hotel. I want to give that feeling to every person who walks into my hotel, comfort that won't get anywhere in the world. And that thing is not here."

Kaishav Jain: "I love your thoughts, your strategy. Wow!! I get it 100%. You have that land itched in your mind, but you don't want to go ahead with it out of fear. You are afraid of something that you have no reason to be afraid of. Let me tell you, Mr Kumar, if you are looking for the same location somewhere else, then sorry to say, it's not possible. If you search all over India, you will not find it. I guarantee you that."

Jaswant Kumar and Kaishav Jain are in the car on their way to Jaisalmer.

Jaswant Kumar: "How can you be so sure he won't get bail?"

Kaishav Jain: "OK, shall I say if the sun does not rise tomorrow, or someone has swallowed the earth? Would you believe it? This is India, not Pakistan; a person who has committed such a crime cannot just get away. Do you not believe in the law of the country?"

Jaswant Kumar: "I am not aware of all these things."

Kaishav Jain: "That's why you are asking the questions. You don't need to worry about anything. You are associated with Jains Real Estate; for us, the safety of our clients is primary."

Location: Government Registration Office, Jaisalmer

Time: 5:00 (Evening)

Kaishav Jain: "Don't go by that old man's words this time; you have to give documents, fill out the form, give the check, and get it done. I am waiting for you here in the car. As said earlier, we do the work professionally, and honestly, you have to pay me 10% of the total amount. The deal is crystal clear."

Jaswant Kumar: "Okay."

Jaswant Kumar re-enters the registration office and waits for his turn.

Chhagan Singh: "You are here again?"

Jaswant Kumar (hesitatingly) – "Sir I… I…"

Chhagan Singh: "No problem, I have verified these documents. Let it be deposited here with me so that I can process it. Madam will give you a form outside on the desk; fill it out and give it to her.

Jaswant Kumar: "How long will it take?"

Chhagan Singh: "The land will be in your name by tomorrow or the day after tomorrow."

Jaswant Kumar: "OK, thank you, Sir."

Chhagan Singh: "Okay then, I wish you all the best for your future plans. May God bless you and help you realize your dream."

Jaswant Kumar walks back to the car where Kaishav Jain is waiting.

Kaishav Jain: "Work done?"

Jaswant Kumar: "Yes, they took the documents. Then I submitted the form, and yes, they accepted the check; anything else?"

Kaishav Jain: "Perfect, think it's done. Now, if you give me 10%, I can relax as well. I think I have shown you enough plots to deserve it, and let me tell you, I haven't worked so hard for any clients before. Now you have given a check for the total amount of 36 lakh 60 thousand, out of which 10 percent would mean 3 lakh 60 thousand. As I said before, I accept cash only."

Jaswant Kumar is prepared; he takes out stacks of notes from a bag and gives them to Kaishav Jain. You can count the notes if you want to, Jaswant tells Kaishav Jain.

Kaishav Jain: "Counting is not done everywhere, Mr. Kumar. There is only one dealer in the whole of Jaisalmer; do you know why? Because I do not open my secret in front of anyone. Is that a tea seller over there or a sweet shop? Perhaps all of them are focused on their customers, but their third eye is on me. I never let this city know how much I earn. To everyone, I look like a poor, door-to-door wandering broker. That's why if someone stands before me today, it is me alone, a lone land broker. This is called business, Mr. Kumar. Like your strategy, I also have some principles. Keep it inside; I will go home and count this money. Shall I drop you at the hotel now?"

Jaswant Kumar: "Is there any psychiatrist here?"

Kaishav Jain: "What? What do you mean?"

Jaswant Kumar: "I mean, a doctor who treats mental illness?"

Kaishav Jain: "Yes, understood. Do you mean you are so overwhelmed with this land purchase that you need to see a shrink? Ha ha ha, just kidding. Ok, so let's go to the most famous doctor of Jaisalmer,

Venue: Beautiful Mind Clinic, Ram Paul, Jaisalmer

Time: 6:30 PM

People come here to be treated by Dr. Girish Patel; the 44-year-old physicalistic is so famous that people come here to be treated from all over Rajasthan. Beautiful mind for a beautiful future," Kaishav boasted.

Jaswant Kumar: "Sounds good."

Kaishav Jain: "Yes, go and speak to the doctor, and if you need anything, remember Kaishav. Whether it is a small task or something really big, it doesn't matter; I can give you any type of support you need. The policy of Jain Real Estates…"

"I think this will need some time; thanks for doing all this for me. I must go now, Jaswant." Kumar said impatiently.

Kaishav Jain: "Sure, see you then. Bye."

Jaswant Kumar enters the swanky client, approaches the smartly dressed receptionist, and asks to see the doctor.

"Do you have an appointment, Sir?" The lady asks curtly.

"No, I don't live here, some referred me to the doctor, and I dropped in."

"Ok… Let me see. You will have to wait 30–40 minutes," she clarifies. "That's fine," Jaswant Kumar confirms.

After waiting for around 45 minutes, he is called into the chamber.

"Can I come in, Sir?"

Dr Girish Patel: "Please come in and have a seat."

Jaswant Kumar enters the large room and sits down in a leather upholstered chair.

Dr Girish Patel: "Can I take 2 minutes if you don't mind?"

"Sure, Sir," Jaswant Kumar says as he studies the tall and lanky man with dusky skin and an intelligent, pleasant face.

Dr Girish Patel: "Sorry, I was just looking at a patient's file; it's a little serious, so… I'm really sorry for the inconvenience."

Jaswant Kumar: "No problem."

Dr Girish Patel: "Great, tell me, what's your name?"

Jaswant Kumar: "Jaswant Kumar."

Dr Girish Patel: "So Jaswant Kumar ji, How can I help you with."

Jaswant Kumar: "Sir, I am a resident of Mumbai. I have come here for business purposes."

Dr Girish Patel: "Nice, you have come from Mumbai. There are a lot of people, a lot of traffic."

Jaswant Kumar: "Yes Sir, it is all normal there."

Dr Girish Patel: "Do you have any business there?"

Jaswant Kumar: "Yes."

Dr Girish Patel: "So relax and tell me your problem; you may consider me a friend."

Jaswant Kumar: "Sir, I do not like anything. The head remains heavy. As if someone has put a burden on the head. Sometimes I am hesitant to even talk to anyone, and I feel scared."

Dr Girish Patel: "How is your sleep at night?"

Jaswant Kumar: "My sleep pattern is disturbed. I can't sleep, and even when I sleep, it comes intermittently."

Dr Girish Patel: "If you feel scared like you said, do you feel scared at night as well, or only during the day?"

Jaswant Kumar: "The feeling is more apparent at night. As if I will die. My treatment was started in Mumbai, but after coming here, I ran out of medicines and thought of consulting a doctor. Now, it's starting to feel worse than before. I literally push myself and get the work done."

Dr Girish Patel: "Since when have you been facing this problem?"

Jaswant Kumar: "Perhaps since the time I started understanding."

Dr Girish Patel: "Anybody else in your house, your family, has this problem?"

Jaswant Kumar: "No"

Dr Girish Patel: "OK, do you drink or smoke?"

Jaswant Kumar: "No, Sir, never."

Dr Girish Patel: "Hmmmm… you need not worry. All your troubles will go away. But there is one condition: you have to take the medicines I give you regularly. This will be a 3 year course. It may seem like a long period of time, but I assure you, you will completely heal by then. Are you permanently planning to stay in Jaisalmer or go back to Mumbai?"

Jaswant Kumar: "I am going to stay here forever. And I will do as you say. I just want to be cured."

Dr Girish Patel: "Right now, I am giving you 2 types of medicines for a month. One of the drugs will give you inner happiness and desire to work and boost your self-confidence. You have to take this in the morning after having your meal. And you have to take the second one at night before dinner; it will help you sleep."

Jaswant Kumar: "OK"

Dr Girish Patel: "Next appointment after 1 month. Pay the fees outside at the reception."

Location: Bhagirath Hotel, Shastri Nagar, Jaisalmer

Time: 8:00 PM

Jaswant Kumar has come with his family to have dinner at Bhagirath Hotel. The hotel and restaurant are preached atop a cliff, giving a beautiful view of the city. The lamps illuminate the restaurant, giving each table and the entire place a dream-like feel.

Vaishali Kumar: "Think once again."

Jaswant Kumar: "About what?"

Vaishali Kumar: "We can do something else; there are many business options. A hotel is not the only option. That too, in the middle of a desert. I find it risky."

A turbaned waiter arrives. "Sir, would you like to order?"

Mihir Kumar: "Papa, I want to have ice cream."

Jaswant Kumar: "Yes, dear, let me see the menu first. Vaishali, should we order Paneer masala."

Vaishali Kumar: "Yes."

Jaswant Kumar: "2 Paneer masala, 6 rotis, and a tweety-fruity- ice cream."

Waiter: "OK, anything else, Sir?"

Mihir Kumar: "A cold drink, please."

Vaishali Kumar: "Mihir, sit quietly."

Jaswant Kumar: "Why are you shouting at the child?" (to the waiter) "Add that to the order, please."

Mihir Kumar: "Thank you, Papa."

As soon as the waiter takes the order and leaves, Jaswant Kumar turns to Vaishali and asks her in a low voice, "Why don't you support me? It's not just a one-off case; this is becoming a habit for you. You always doubt me, no matter what I do or how hard I try."

"It is a question of our future. We have come here, leaving everything behind. If this does not succeed, then nothing will be left to us. I don't care about myself, but I care about him, Mihir. I am not stopping you from entering the hotel business; all I am saying is to choose the place wisely where there are people and businesses.

"Vaishali, you have to trust me. I am 55 years old; I am mature enough to make a decision. Believe me, I am weighed the pros and cons before stepping ahead. I am as much concerned about Mihir as you are. Whatever I am doing or will do in the future, it is all for the good of both of you. I know in what condition we left our family, our home. What do you think? I will forget all that. No. Never. I promise I will not let you or Mihir suffer even an inch. You know, dear, for me, my family is everything."

Venue: Prembaba Guest House, Amar Sagar, Paul, Jaisalmer

Time: 11:00 PM

The family is in bed, and while Mihir is fast asleep, Vaishali and Jaswant Kumar are still awake.

"Are you asleep?" Vaishali asks, staring at the ceiling.

Jaswant Kumar: "No, I can smell something really weird."

"Yes, I was about to say that," Vaishali says, trying to sniff the stale air.

Jaswant Kumar looks up at the ceiling and finds a damp spot. Drops of water are leaking through the ceiling.

"What the hell? I think there is a leakage in the pipeline. I am going down to the reception and see what can be done."

Jaswant Kumar hurries down the stairs and reaches the reception.

The reception and the restaurant are in the same hall. There is a crowd of late-night diners loitering around the place.

Jaswant Kumar walks up to the receptionists.

"Sir, there is a pipeline leakage in room 206. Please…"

Receptionist: "Yes, Sir?"

Jaswant Kumar: "There is a leakage in room no. 206."

The receptionist turns his attention to the waiter, "Hey Raj, Table No. 7 is complaining. Where is their order? Move your ass, hurry up."

Jaswant waits patiently for the receptionist to finish, and by the time he is free, he looks at Jaswant Kumar again and asks, quizzically, "Yes, Sir, your meal?

"Sir, water is dripping from the ceiling of our room. We are not able to sleep. The whole room is stinking… can you please do something about it?"

Receptionist: "Okay, you go upstairs, I'll send the plumber right now."

Jaswant Kumar: "Thank you. Please make it quick."

Jaswant Kumar goes up to his room and assures Vaishali that the plumber is on his way. Half an hour later, the stink had gotten worse, and the droplets were falling with more regularity with no sign of the plumber.

"Enough is enough; we have paid for this room. Why should we take such nonsense?" Vaishali fumes.

"Where are you going?" Jaswant Kumar asks.

"Either you go to the reception, or I must go now. How can they be so irresponsible…"

Jaswant Kumar: "Wait, I will go; these people did not pay heed to my civil behavior. Now it's time to try another method."

Receptionist: "Yes, Sir."

Jaswant Kumar: "I told you half an hour earlier that drain water is leaking from the ceiling; no one has come to fix it yet."

Receptionist: "Oh! Yes," he turns at a man standing a little farther away. "Arree, I told you about it such long ago. Should I use a loudspeaker now? Where is your bloody attention? Go to room No. 206 right now and check the row of pipes, find the leakage, and fix it."

Jaswant Kumar: "Sure?"

By now, the receptionist has turned his attention back to the restaurant billing.

Jaswant Kumar returns to the room. Vaishali has put a bucket under the leakage area, so the water doesn't spread on the floor.

Vaishali: "What happened?"

"Now even his shadow will come. I gave him an earful and created a scene, and everyone was looking. I told him if he could not fix the problem right now, I would take strict action against him."

Vaishali: "Really?"

"Absolutely, I told him, if he had it fixed earlier, there wouldn't have been so much trouble."

Vaishali: "Jasu, I have known you for 30 years. You are no man to quarrel over such a matter, so please stop lying."

Time: 1:00 AM

Vaishali and their son Mihir have gone to sleep. But Jaswant Kumar cannot sleep because of the sound of the falling droplets and the stink. Exasperated, Jaswant Kumar gets up and takes out foil paper from his bag and a handkerchief. He pulls a chair as noiselessly as he can, tiptoes over it, and tries to fix the area, sticking the handkerchief and foil paper with some chewing gum. Finally, the water stops dripping, being soaked by the handkerchief and held in place by the gum and foil paper.

Jaswant Kumar tries to sleep, but sleep deludes him. After tossing and turning in bed, he notices that the pasted paper gives way, and water starts dripping again. Jaswant Kumar lies with his eyes wide open. The sound of dripping water echoes in his ears, creating chaos. Maybe I should have booked a better hotel. His mind wanders off to his own hotel dream; a bright future awaits him… but he can't keep the dark thoughts at bay…

Did he make the right decision? Is purchasing the land a good decision? Who is Kalu Singh? What if he turns out to be a threat?

How will it affect the lives intertwined with the land? These are thoughts that keep him awake till the wee hours…

Chapter 2

The Titan Model

A Day Before the Present

Jaswant Kumar takes out 4 heavy bags from his rented back sedan one by one and hands over 2 bags to the young man standing beside him. Then he wraps the strap of 1 bag on his right shoulder and carries the other in his left hand. Now, the duo stares at each other for a brief moment and, without exchanging any words, walks toward the four-story, white-washed building that houses the office they are meant to be at.

Location: 7B, Shastri Nagar, Jaisalmer

Time: 8:30 (Next Morning)

Kaishav Jain: "Just look at this gorgeous house. A house fit for a King. You won't find such a luxurious and comfortable house in the entire Jaisalmer."

He walks around the house, leading the way as Vaishali, Mihir, and Jaswant follow. 3 large bedrooms, a kitchen, and a tiny lawn overlooking the hall.

Jaswant looked outside; he wondered if the tiny patch of green, maybe 60-70 square feet at the most, could be called a lawn.

"What else do you want?" Kaishav Jain continues… "Bhabhi, tell me what you feel."

Vaishali: "It looks fine."

Kaishav Jain: "See, I know Bhabhi has an excellent choice; in fact, her choice is so good, I think she should be somewhere else, making choices and decisions like some politician. Haha, just kidding!"

Jaswant: "The house is fine, but what is the rent?"

Kaishav Jain: "Only 40 thousand per month."

Jaswant: "That's too much."

Kaishav Jain: "Oh, come on, Mr. Kumar, the amount is nothing compared to the house. To top it off, this is a well-to-do, decent neighborhood. All residences nearby belong to doctors and top businessmen, and yes, it's a safe locality. Even if you go out of town, you don't have to worry about your family."

Little Mihir looks out of the window at the patch of green, "Papa, this house is good."

Kaishav – "Look, you have a family. That's why it is essential to see the locality. And you know me, I will never direct you to the wrong place or give you the wrong advice.

Jaswant Kumar: "Okay. But I can't spend more than 35 thousand of this."

Kaishav Jain: "OK, let's strike a deal at 38 thousand. OK?"

Jaswant Kumar reluctantly agrees, "Once we have a deal, I will need to see everything."

Jaswant Kumar: " Also, please ensure we meet the landlord, and I would like to have an agreement in place."

Kaishav Jain: "Leave all that to me. The demand of the house owner is high; I will have to convince him. Also, as per the owner's terms, you will have to pay 2 lakhs, and the agreement period tenure will be at least 1 year."

Jaswant: Sounds fine; let's move on it as fast as we can.

Kaishav: " From today, this house is yours. Do whatever you want, and Mr. Kumar, you can rest now, but think about me. I, too, need to rest."

Jaswant: "Yes, understood." Jaswant Kumar takes out money from the bag.

Kaishav Jain: "No, don't give this here."

Jaswant Kumar and Kaishav Jain are sitting inside the car in the silent wiz of the air-conditioner. He keeps the money given by Jaswant Kumar in his bag.

"By the way, the money you gave yesterday was less than 500 rupees."

Jaswant: "I gave you after counting, and I asked you to count too.

"This is against my principles," Kaishav quips.

Jaswant: "When do you think the land papers will arrive? I am waiting for the land to be legally mine so that I can start with the project."

Kaishav Jain: "Don't worry, this land is the governments. You will get the registration paper by today or tomorrow."

Jaswant: "Can you also put me in touch with a good architect?"

"Yes, that too can be arranged. When Jain Real Estate is there for you, there is possibly nothing you can't have."

"By now, I mean today," Jaswant Kumar says, cutting off Kaishav's banter.

"Today? You are not willing to wait for anything, right? You move like a Bullet Train… And you command like a Nazi," … Kaishav mocks.

"Why do you have to twist everything? I have asked a direct question; if you know someone, please contact me. Can you do that? "

Kaishav Jain: "Yes, yes, I know just the right person for you. Let me fix this: exactly an hour from now, stand at Panchnada Chauraha. You will have your man."

Location: Panchnada Chauraha., Jaisalmer

Time: 10:35 AM

Jaswant had been waiting at the crossroads, under a police kiosk for some time now, amidst the honking and traffic snarls. Then Jaswant notices a young man on a bike staring here and there. Then he arrives at the crossroads. Jaswant Kumar walks up to him and asks… has Kaishav Jain sent you?"

The young man nods in affirmative and extends his hand, Mr. Kumar? Right? I am Bindu.

The traffic sergeant at the kiosk blows his whistle and directs the men to move away.

Bindu: Sir, hop on.

Jaswant Kumar: "On the bike?"

Bindu: "It's a little old, but don't worry, it will take you to the right place"

Location: Jaisalmer – Munabao Road

Time: 12:00 (Noon)

Bindu is riding the bike with Jaswant Kumar at the back. As they leave the city behind, the houses disappear, and there are small patches of green here and there amidst the huge expanse of sand. Occasionally, a truck or a car passes them, but mostly, the road is empty. The asphalt glows in the extreme heat, and the occasional gust of wind that hits them as they ride is almost unbearable.

Bindu: "How far is it?"

Jaswant Kumar: "I think it will take an hour from here."

Bindu: "Any particular reason why you choose a place so far away from the city?"

Jaswant ignores Bindu's question and asks– "Are you from Jaisalmer?"

Bindu: "No, Sir. I am from Bhavnagar, Gujarat. It's been a year since I have been here,"

Jaswant Kumar: "So, what are your credentials? Did you train to be an architect?

Bindu: "Sir, I have done a Diploma in Engineering."

Jaswant Kumar: "So, have you worked anywhere before? On any real projects?"

Bindu: "No, Sir, not in that sense. This is going to be my first."

Jaswant Kumar remains silent.

Location: 17+69, 34+42, 04+23

Time: 1:30 PM

Bindu: "Wow!! This place looks so different, cool."

Jaswant Kumar: "Yes, I want to build a hotel here."

Bindu: "What!! Here you want to build a hotel, I mean here?

Jaswant Kumar: "I want to do something different. Not just a usual hotel. I want to build a world-class hotel here. Have you heard of Burj Al Arab Jumeirah or the Taj Lake Palace in Lake Pichola, Udaipur? These are iconic hotels that people dream of visiting, and I want to build a hotel like that. An entity that people will relate with luxury and grandeur. People like to see what they have not seen anywhere else, something out of the world. And I will create just that: an iconic hotel."

Bindu: "Wow! You have some vision. What's the total area of the property you wish to build on?

Jaswant Kumar: "As much empty ground as you can see right now. About 7 acres."

Bindu: "So you will build a hotel on about 7 acres?"

Jaswant Kumar: "Yes"

Bindu: "Sir, I see you have a grand vision, but isn't 7 acres a lot of land? So much area is befitting an industry or factory. I know I am too young to give advice, but still. Moreover, it is not easy to set up such a big project, and that too in such a desolate area. It will cost a lot of money. A lot."

Jaswant Kumar: "Yes, maybe you are too young and inexperienced to visualize this. Just tell me whether you can do it or not."

Bindu: "Sir, if you have the resources. Then I can tell you this will be the eighth wonder of the world, and I will consider myself lucky that I will be a part of this phenomenal project. Sir, I will make it grand beyond your imagination."

Jaswant Kumar: "Tell me one thing: do you know any good contractors or teams you can deploy on the job?"

Bindu: "Sir, I work alone right now, but I can arrange for contractors, laborers…"

Jaswant Kumar: "Then how will you be able to do all this? I am not very sure now. This project will need manpower and years of experience."

Bindu: "Sir, I agree that I do not have experience. But I can say this much: I can create the world you have imagined. I will workday and night to make this happen. I will make your dream my own. Also, I know a person who can supply all the construction materials and workers."

Jaswant Kumar: "Can you give a rough estimate of the total expenditure?"

Bindu: "Sir, give me time till tonight. Will tell you after doing my complete calculation."

Location: 7B, Shastri Nagar, Jaisalmer

Time: 8:30 PM

Jaswant enters his new residence and is surprised to see everything set up. The house that he had left this morning in a state of disarray is now looking like a perfect home, all furniture set up at their rightful places, and an air-conditioner in the bedroom, a television in the sitting room…

The scent of fried masala was wafting through the air, and sure enough, Vaishali was busy in the kitchen. Mihir is so engrossed in watching cartoons he hardly notices when his Papa comes in. Jaswant: "Beta, you should cut down on that cartoon!"

Vaishali: "Oh, you have come just in time; I was making dinner. Tell me, how did your day go?"

Jaswant Kumar: "Well, I talked to a young guy sent by Kaishav; let's see what comes of it. But you tell me how you managed to do all this by yourself. Who helped you arrange the furniture and set up the house?

Kaishav Jain sent in a man who brought in some fresh vegetables, arranged all the furniture, helped me set up the kitchen, carried a gas cylinder into it, even hung the curtains, and sprinkled the ground outside with water."

"Glad to know that someone was there to help you. Thank God we found Kaishav Jain; otherwise, Jaisalmer wouldn't have been so easy to settle in," Jaswant said as he sat down on the sofa.

Vaishali: "Well, he may be our man Friday, but he has a price for everything; the man overcharged the vegetables, almost double the price, and after each service, there is a bill."

Jaswant Kumar: "Well, don't worry, dear, I know he overcharges, but at least the work is being done."

The doorbell rings. Jaswant Kumar opens the door. A man dressed in work clothes stands at the door, "Namaste Sir, Jain Sir has sent this for you."

Jaswant Kumar takes the envelope in his hand, opens it, and starts reading it.

Jaswant: "Hey, listen up, Vaishali, the registration is done. The land is now officially ours."

Vaishali: (screams in happiness) "Really!"

Jaswant: "Yes, Yes, the first step of this venture is accomplished; we are good to get started."

Later that night, around 12.40 am. when Jaswant is finally sleeping peacefully, medicated, in his new home, his cell phone rings. Groggy from sleep, he picks up the phone after quite a few rings.

"Sir, I have done all the calculations, and according to them, it will cost 46 crores. Hello?"

There is silence.

Bindu: "Sir, I know the cost is high, but it is the least for what you want to make. I will keep my profit next to nothing. Sir, since you have told me about the idea, I am married to this project, and I will make it happen just the way you want it. You there, Sir?"

Jaswant collects his bearing and answers… "It is 1 o'clock in the night; I was sleeping. Can we talk tomorrow?"

Bindu: "Oh, yes. Sorry, Sir, I shouldn't have called at this time. I… I was really so excited I lost track of time.

Location: 512, Gandhi Nagar, Jaisalmer

Time: 1:00 AM

Bindu is drawing the hotel's diagram when he gets distracted by the sound of something falling. Bindu gets up and goes to the room to check on his father. A thin, pale man of 75 who has been bedridden for quite some time now. He has sharp, pleasant features, resembling his son, but years of illness have created hollows under his eyes.

Bindu: "What are you doing, Papa? He notices the steel glass on the floor.

"You could have called me?"

"You were working, and I didn't want to disturb you, son."

Bindu picks up another glass and pours water for his father, "And did you take the medicine?"

"Of course I did. Now, you don't overwork; you should go to sleep now."

Bindu: "I have got a big project; for the first time in my life, how can I sleep?"

As Bindu turns to switch off the lights, he notices some wood panels lying on the side of the room and some thermocol sheets.

Location: Shastri Nagar, Jaisalmer

Time: 9:00 (Next Morning)

Jaswant Kumar is waiting for a rickshaw at Shastri Nagar Square.

He waves down a rikshaw and asks, "Maheshwari Agency, Shanipar Chowk?"

The rickshaw puller quoted his price, and Jaswant hopped on, trying to make himself comfortable on the red and blue seat. Right at that moment, the phone rings.

Bindu: "Hi, Sir. Where are you?"

Jaswant: "I am still busy with work; let's talk later."

Bindu: "Don't hang up the phone, Sir. Can you come to my house now? I have something to show you."

Jaswant Kumar: "I can't come now. I have some work…"

Bindu: "Sir, I will not waste a moment of your time. Please, Sir, I want to show you something."

Jaswant Kumar: "What thing?"

Bindu: "I can't tell you on the phone; you must see this. My address is Teesri Galli, 512, Gandhi Nagar. I will be waiting for you."

"Can you take me to Teesri Galli, 512, Gandhi Nagar?" Jaswant asks the rickshaw puller.

"Sabh, it's in the wrong direction; how can you ask me to change the direction like this? I chose you because I was heading to my nearby house. Now, you're telling me to turn around and go back?"

Jaswant: "It's an emergency. I have to be there."

"Why didn't you tell me earlier? I would have refused then and there. I will need at least 80 rupees extra." the rickshaw puller grumbles.

"I will give you the extra money. Just take me there. Anyway, ever since I came to this city, It has become a habit to pay extra money," Jaswant Kumar.

Time: 9:30 AM

Jaswant Kumar reaches the address; it is a small one-storied house with a small courtyard among a row of similar-looking houses, only this one looks a little run down. He knocks on the green wooden painted door.

Bindu opens the door almost instantly. "Welcome, Sir, please come inside."

The inside of the house is in a state of disarray, things strewn here and there; Bindu takes out a chair, wipes off the dust with his hand, and asks Jaswant to sit.

Before Jaswant gets a chance to say anything, Bindu disappears into the house and reappears with a glass of water on a plastic tray. Sir, can I get you tea, or should I make coffee?

Jaswant: "No, no, I am in a hurry. So, this is where you live? Jaswant asked, looking around the house."

Bindu: "Yes, Sir, I am afraid it is in a mess, but this is my house. I am not a wealthy man, but I can fend for myself and take care of myself and my aging father."

An old man from inside the house… "Who is it, son?"

Bindu: "No one, Papa, it is my boss."

"Sir, that is my father. He is not well; in fact, he can't walk." …Jaswant interrupts him impatiently… "Bindu, I really have to go somewhere, so please, if you can tell me what I am here for…"

"Oh yes, I will show you…" Bindu takes Jaswant Kumar to a room. An old cloth covers something on a table. Bindu gently picks up the cloth, revealing a miniature model of the hotel, complete with gardens, pools, several buildings, and tree-lined paths connecting one portion with the other.

Jaswant stares at the model: Impressive!

Bindu: "Look at this, Sir. Our hotel will look like this: amazing, right? Just like the top hotels in the world.

7 acres of divine space. And, Sir, I have thought of its name too. The Titan Hotel, you know what Titan means, right? Biggest, strongest, and extraordinary someone or something that no storm in the world can shake or uproot. So, tell me, how did you like my model?"

Jaswant: "Good, but you made all this? I mean, we just spoke yesterday, and I haven't yet confirmed you for the job. "

Bindu: "Yes, Sir, I had the material at home, a little paint, thermocol, and a bunch of wooden sticks, so I created this model according to the diagram."

Jaswant: "So, did you spend the whole night making this!!"

Bindu quietly replies, "Yes, Sir."

Jaswant: "Good; in fact, I find this model a superb interpretation of my dream. But Bindu, sorry to say my project is huge, and it will require very experienced engineers, architects, and professional skills. Yes, I know you will get this done by a builder, but you don't have any experience, and let me tell you, getting a structure of this massive scale up and running is no child's play. Do you understand what I am saying?"

Bindu: "Sir, that experience doesn't need to be required for every work. Sir, I have a vision… Jaswant cut off the conversation: "I appreciate your efforts, but I want to go with someone with some experience."

Bindu (his face crestfallen) – "No problem, Sir. Do as you feel is right."

Jaswant: "Thank you, thank you for understanding my situation. And I'm so glad you made this model for me."

"It wasn't for you, Sir; it was for the hotel. The dream you showed me yesterday I have adopted as my own."

Jaswant Kumar: "Thank you for whatever you did, and I would really like to pay for this model."

Bindu: "No Sir, I don't want money. You said that you like it; that is enough for me."

Location: Maheshwari Agency, Shanipar Chowk, Jaisalmer

Time: 10:30 AM

Jaswant Kumar is waiting in the air-conditioned lobby of Maheshwari Agencies, waiting to meet Mr. Rahul Sinha. After a while, the desk clerk asks him to go inside.

"May I come in, Sir?"

Rahul Sinha, the proprietor, is a man in his mid-thirties, bespectacled, fair-complexioned, and of medium build.

"Oh, of course. Please have a seat."

Jaswant Kumar: "Sir, I have come from Mumbai and…

Rahul Sinha: "No need to tell me your background; I am a little rushed, so can we come straight to the point? Have you brought the land documents?"

Jaswant Kumar: "Yes, here you are."

Rahul Sinha: (while looking at the documents) Hmmm, so you want to build a hotel here, right? Ok. Let me tell you; we have some ongoing work, big contracts like mills, highways, government projects, hospitals, etc. So, this is not going to be a priority project for us. By the way, did you consider anyone else for this job?"

Jaswant Kumar: "Yes, a young architect named Bindu."

Rahul Sinha: "Sorry to interrupt you, but what was his name, 'Bindu'?" Did you go to him? He is a kid, and till today, he hasn't designed a room, and you considered him. (Laughing). Thank God, you realized your mistake and came to us. I assure you; you have come to the right place."

Jaswant Kumar: "Sir, what will be its budget?"

Rahul Sinha: "I can't tell you the exact number, but the budget will be approximately 35 crores."

Jaswant Kumar: "OK" I don't have a problem with that; I just want the best for this project."

Rahul Sinha: "Ok. So, your next appointment will be the second of next month."

Jaswant Kumar: "Sir, why next month?"

Rahul Sinha: "We already have many projects underway, government projects which are very important for us. And your work, I dare say, is smaller in comparison. And another thing, we do our work according to our priority, so if something very important comes in the way, we might just be a little delayed on your project."

Jaswant Kumar: "Sir, can you please return these documents?"

Rahul Sinha: "What happened?"

Jaswant Kumar: "If I can't measure up to your high standard and the project seems insignificant to you, then let it be. I will find someone who values my project. Goodbye."

Jaswant Kumar comes out of the Maheshwari Agencies building, takes out the phone from his pocket, and dials Bindu's number.

"What are you doing?"

Bindu: "Just sitting around, Sir."

Jaswant Kumar: "I think it's time we get down to work."

Bindu: "I don't understand, Sir; you said I am not fit for this job…"

Jaswant Kumar: "Maybe I was wrong; maybe you are my man after all… I've realized that you have passion, and I think only you can do this. The time has arrived, so get ready for an epic ride; here we go…"

Chapter 3

Here We Go!

Bank officials take out stacks of notes from the vault. 6 money-counting machines are kept on 2 tables; the cash is to be counted, regrouped into stacks of 10 thousand, and handed over to the client. After a final check, the neatly banded notes are carefully arranged into 4 separate bags.

Location: Bank of India, Jaisalmer

Time: 9:30 AM

Jaswant Kumar and Kaishav Jain are sitting inside the manager's cabin. 4 bags, filled with the money, are brought in from the interior of the office.

"Sir, you have brought a car."

Jaswant: "Yes, there is a white car parked beside the gate; the number is 4201. Please ask your staff to load the bags in the trunk. Let me take them to the car…"

The bank security guard picks up all 4 bags and puts them in the trunk of the car. Jaswant Kumar and Kaishav Jain get into the car once the money is loaded.

"May the tire avoid popping from the pressure – my car might not be a Ferrari, but with all this cash on board, I'm starting to think I accidentally bought a money magnet on wheels!" Kaishav Jain laughs.

"Yes. Can I really believe that? It's not a joke; I still have doubts," Jaswant reflects.

Kaishav Jain: "Ah, I am Kaishav Jain, the man who doesn't believe in second thoughts, just straight into action! But these actions are dependent according to the situation. And come on, he's, my man. Bindu, don't worry, Mr. Kumar, this Kaishav takes full care of its clients; you will get what you want…"

Location: 512, Gandhi Nagar, Jaisalmer

Time: 10:00 AM

Kaishav Jain: "We have reached; let's get the bags out of the car."

Jaswant Kumar: "OK, help me."

Kaishav Jain: "Seriously!! Now, you want me to work like this? … OK. Only for you, Mr Kumar."

They take out the bags from the trunk, and each carry 2 bags and places them on the doorstep.

Kaishav Jain: "OK, my responsibility is over now. Wish you a wonderful day ahead, bye.

Jaswant Kumar: "Where are you going?"

"I am going to a children's park to get on a swing and enjoy the rest of the day there…" Kaishav says sarcastically. I, too, have important work to take care of; there are clients like you for whom I have to fulfill their needs, and I have to handle them and keep them happy. If they are happy, there's more money."

Kaishav Jain leaves in his car, and Jaswant Kumar knocks on the green-painted door. Bindu opens doors.

"Welcome, Sir; please come inside."

Jaswant Kumar: "Will you help me carry these bags?"

"Of Course,"

All the 4 bags are brought into the house.

"The bag is very heavy; what is in it?" Bindu asks with concern.

Jaswant Kumar: "Money."

Bindu "Money?"

Jaswant Kumar: "Each bag has 2 crores, so 4 bags have 8 crores."

"Hmm, a lot of cash," Bindu says as he keeps the bags in one corner of the room.

"There is a total of 8 crores in those bags. Can you please consider this as the advance fee for the builder? Work on the project will have to start immediately."

Bindu: "You are right; we have to start immediately. But Sir, I have told you earlier, this builder is pretty big, and his condition is to get the full payment upfront. They have some rules, and full payment before work commencement is one of them."

"I cannot withdraw the entire amount from the bank at once," Jaswant says, a little worried, "and usually, such huge payments are made in installments only."

Bindu: "Okay, let me see what I can do."

Jaswant Kumar: "Now everything is in your hand, as I thought it should be made according to my imagination. I want the workmanship to be of a high standard; otherwise, I assure you there will be no shortage of funds from my side. But do ensure the quality of work is of the highest level."

"Sir, you have put your trust in me, and I will give my hundred percent and some more to live up to that," Bindu says.

Location: Joseph Property Construction Lines, Jaisalmer

Time: 10:00 AM

Jaswant Kumar takes out 4 heavy bags from his rented back sedan one by one and hands over 2 bags to the young man standing Bindu. Then he wraps the strap of one bag on his right shoulder and carries the other one in his left hand. Now, the duo stares at each other for a brief moment and, without exchanging any words, walks toward the four-story, white-washed building that houses the office they are meant to be at.

Bindu: "Sir, I will go and meet Mr. Robert; and see if I can fix a deal. You wait outside for a while. I just went and just came back."

Bindu carries the 2 bags inside and then appears again to get the rest 2. Robert is a tall and well-built man in his late forties. In the business world, he is often referred to as Don Robert. He owns the entire office building, but he is usually found in his first-floor office sitting on a leather upholstered chair in front of a large Mahagony desk. Bindu has to seek the help of a guard to get the bags inside.

Bindu precariously knocks on the door and enters the room… Don Robert is wearing a black shirt with the front buttons undone to show his well-toned chest. He is wearing at least 3 or 4 gaudy gold chains around his neck. 2 muscular bodyguards are standing behind his chair. "Oh, my God! Look who has come! Bindu!"

"Hello, Robert Sir."

"Hey, my child. What brings you here after such a long time?" (he turns to one of the bodyguards and orders him, "Get 2 cups of Malai chai."

"Tell me, Bindu, what's in those bags?"

Bindu; "Sir, I have come to make a deal with you."

"Deal? What kind of deal?"

"There is a project. Hotel Construction, and I want to give you the contract if you are interested."

Don Robert: "Bindu, my child, you know I don't do small things."

Bindu: "Sir, trust me, this work is huge. The project is to be built on 7 acres of land. The client has very high standards, and he wants to build a luxury hotel of its kind. I have estimated around 46 crores expenses."

Don Robert: "What did you say? Say it again."

Bindu: "46 crores!"

"Son, how did you get such a huge deal? Wow. (Looking at the bodyguard) Didn't I say that one day, this guy will do something worthwhile?" The Don says, laughing in excitement. "Tell me more about it!"

Bindu: "Sir, as I said, this is going to be a luxurious hotel, one of its kind, think seven-star. The client demands that the material used in construction should be of high quality. I have already panned the interiors, but the stuff used in it should also be of standard material. And I know you are the only one in the whole world who can pull off this huge task."

Don Robert: "Son, there are many builders in this country who reach the top level. I am one of them. I didn't get my name just like that; I earned it through hard work. From the USA and Mexico to Japan and Australia, I am recognized everywhere. Every product used in this project will be the best product in the world.

But the whole game is about money; I hope you realize that."

Bindu: "Yes, Sir, here is 8 crores, advance."

Don Robert: "8 crores? What will happen with 8 crores?"

Bindu: "Sir, only advance; the client will keep paying once the work starts."

"Ah! You know all these advances don't work for me. Throw away all the money. And it will cost me 50 crores. Will he be able to pay more? Don Robert asks, squinting his eyes."

"Sir, the client can't withdraw such a huge amount from the bank all at once. You know that there is a risk of investigation in this. Please, Sir, accept this; your money will go nowhere. Trust me."

Don Robert: "Okay, I take your word for it, and I am glad that at least you are getting some good work. Now, listen carefully. The contract for this project will be valid for 1.5 years. You have given me 8 crores. Now 42 crores will have to be paid within this period. That means 2 crore 80 thousand should reach me every month. You know very well I don't work like this, taking money in installments, but for you, I am agreeing."

Bindu: "Sir, I don't know how to thank you for this."

Don Robert: "My whole business is based on word of mouth, on mutual trust. You know I stick to my words, and I will want you and your client to do the same. He says, "We have a deal. Leave behind the site area details and address of the client. The engineering team will reach the construction site exactly 10 days from today.""

Bindu comes out of the office.

Jaswant Kumar: "What happened?"

"As you said… Here we go!" Bindu smiles happily.

10 Days Later

Date: 25/09/2009

Location: 17+69, 34+42, 04+23

Time: 3:00 PM

Jaswant Kumar stares at the expansive acreage of land that he owns with pride… Modern machines are digging the field, and 17 rakes have arrived carrying cement, concrete, iron bars, stones, and other goods. 6 tankers full of water are coming. workers and 32 engineers are engaged on the job- work-in-progress.

Bindu: "Sir, where the excavation is going on, there will be our main building structure, and on the far-left side over, there will be the garden; the back of the main building will have the first pool, the lawn…

Jaswant Kumar: "Yes, Yes, I have seen the plan so many times, and now it's itched in my memory. Tell me, Bindu, in how many days will the hotel be ready?"

"Sir, as you can see, we are trying to work as fast and best we can, but it will take at least one and a half years to complete."

Jaswant Kumar: "One and half years? Are you sure? How will all this happen in one and a half years?"

Bindu: "Sir, work will continue day and night. See there, Bindu said, pointing his finger to the far end of the site; they are erecting tents there. All the workers and supervisors will stay here. Till it is fully complete, their residence is here; they will work, eat, and sleep here."

Jaswant Kumar: "How many rooms will be there?"

Bindu: "At present, there are 250, but this number may increase. Sir, this site will be like a mini-village until the work is complete."

Bindu's eyes fall on a man, and he rushes to get his attention.

"Jaswant, Sir, please meet our head civil engineer; he is foreseeing all the civil construction here."

"Hi, my name is Arun Shukla," the man says, extending his hand.

Jaswant shakes his hand. "Hello, Mr. Shukla."

"Sir, here is Jaswant Kumar, the owner of this project."

Arun Shukla: "Oh, Sir, I am so pleased to meet you."

Bindu: "Excuse me, I will have to leave now; you 2, please carry on."

Arun Shukla: "So, Sir, what do you think of the progress?"

Jaswant Kumar: "How many meters do you have to dig up to start work?"

"Since the ground is a flat minimum of 20 feet," Arun Shukla says.

Jaswant Kumar: "Why 20 feet? As far as I know, 7 to 8 feet of foundation should be enough."

Arun Shukla: "We are making underground rooms as per the blueprint, so it's not your usual foundation. By the way, Sir, your architect has shaped the structure in a very creative way. It's very impressive."

Jaswant Kumar: "You think so? Can you tell me about the construction process?"

"From cement to iron bars, everything is being used of premium quality. Special Jodhpuri stones will be used for the foundation of the hotel building, and all the products are strong and durable, so you don't have to worry about repair or renovation. We don't want to compromise on the quality," Arun explains.

Date: 20/09/2010

Location: 17+69, 34+42, 04+23

Time: 10:00 (Morning)

Jaswant Kumar and Bindu are now standing in front of the structure.

Bindu: "How do you feel, Sir?"

Jaswant Kumar: "It is beyond even my expectations. Really, you have honored my trust."

Bindu: "We both have made this together, Sir."

Jaswant Kumar: "I wonder how the interior will turn out to be? The exterior looks amazing. I can only imagine when the pool is full and the lawn is lush, and grand all this will look especially during the dusk."

Bindu: "Sir, I assure you the interior will be so grand that everyone will be fascinated by it. I will use Burma Teak wood for the furniture, which is being imported from Myanmar, while superior quality glass is being brought in from Belgium for doors and mirrors. We are getting the marbles from Italy, and the floor will be covered by special Jaipur velvet carpets. I plan to create an opulent Royal look. Come, I will show you the work-in-progress."

Jaswant Kumar and Bindu are standing on the ground floor of the main hotel building.

Bindu: "Sir, we will have our reception here just as you walk through the main gate. This hall will be 6 thousand square feet. The reception desk will be a combination of Burma Teak and Italian marble top. There will be rows of luxury sofas for the customers to sit and chill. There will be a few storerooms next to the reception. A big chandelier will be installed at the center of the hall. Sir, I plan to install 25 chandeliers across the floors. At least one hundred and 20 pots and vases are being made to decorate the outdoor and indoor spaces. There will be a garden in the middle of the hotel. And as you can see, the main building of the hotel will be taller than the Jasasamgam temple.

Now, Sir, allow me the privilege of showing you around the rooms."

Jaswant Kumar and Bindu enter one of the suite rooms… "Sir, all the suite rooms are 1600 sq. feet each. Sir, from basic amenities like air-conditioners, mini-bar, workstations, etc, there will be a walking closet, a separate living area, a kitchenette, and a bedroom. But the best part of the rooms is, well, you have to see this for yourself." He takes Jaswant to a massive picture window, which gives a splendid view of the desert.

"Sir, the bathroom will be as exclusive as can be with all modern amenities, and the bath will overlook the desert as well so that guests can enjoy the view while taking a bubble bath and sipping champagne! And this facility and size will be made available in each and every room. There will be a total of 250 rooms in the entire hotel. Out of them, 84 rooms will be in the underground basement, but I have designed it as such that they will each have a window overlooking the hotel grounds."

Jaswant Kumar: "Can't believe this is your first job."

Bindu:"Thanks, Sir. The painting will start in just 2 days. Once all the paint is done, the delivery and installation of the rest of the material will start."

Jaswant Kumar:"Hmmm."

"And Sir, I wanted to remind you that your next installment is due in the next 2 days."

Jaswant Kumar: "Bindu, all this is very good, but stop the work at the south-eastern side of the plot where you want to make that traditional wall installation with a lotus pond. I think that section can wait. I am facing a slight investment problem."

Bindu: "Sir, the work on the hotel is 90% complete. Don't you think leaving that part will impact the grand look we are trying to create for the outdoors?"

Jaswant Kumar: "The cost of the interior is very high. Right now, I do not have the budget to complete the entire process. We are already investing a lot for the interiors; I am afraid I won't be able to pull off expenses for other non-essential sections right now, so that is why I am saying stop the outdoor work for the time being. The pool and the gardens are already done, so the hotel will get its desired look and feel."

Bindu: "OK, but you will have to pay the installment to the builder; otherwise, things might get a little difficult with him. The upcoming expenses may not be huge, but the expenses that have been incurred will have to be paid."

Jaswant Kumar: "Don't worry about that; after 2 days, you will get the money."

Location: 7B, Shastri Nagar, Jaisalmer

Time: 10:00 PM

Mihir Kumar leaves his toy as soon as he hears the car pull up in the driveway and rushes to greet him, "Papa…"

Jaswant Kumar picks him up in his arms and asks, "How was your day, beta?"

Vaishali Kumar: "He keeps playing with his friend all day long."

Jaswant Kumar: "If he doesn't play now, when will he play, when he is in my age? Am I right, son?"

Mihir Kumar puts his hands around his head and says– "I love you, Papa."

"I love you too, beta."

Vaishali: "Come on, it's time to sleep now; go to bed. Papa is tired; let him catch his breath, now get off him."

"Ok, Mom, I will listen to you, but promise you will make Maggie for my breakfast?"

"Yes, Yes. Now go," Vaishali says, nudging him on the back.

"Thank you, maa, good night, Papa."

Jaswant Kumar: "Good night, son."

Once Mihir leaves for bed, Vaishali asks, "Why are you so late? Tell me, how is the hotel coming along?"

Jaswant Kumar: "It is almost done. Now it is only a matter of a few more months."

Vaishali Kumar: "Can't wait for it to be completed. Please freshen up, and I will heat the dinner…"

Date – 02/03/2011

Location: 17+69, 34+42, 04+23

Time: 2:30 PM

Bindu: "Sir, we have a problem, a water supply issue. I have calculated we need 2100 liters of water daily, and it is a difficult task to make this available in this desert area… Jaisalmer is 100 kilometers from here, and there is no village nearby."

Jaswant Kumar: "Bindu, I had thought about this problem and then a solution a year ago. We have to make underground storage, storage that can store several gallons of water for at least a month. When the tank is empty, we will order water tankers from Jaisalmer for a refill."

Sounds great; Bindu says, "Sir, we are installing solar panels on the roof of the hotel so that there is no problem with electricity."

Jaswant Kumar: "Most importantly, CCTV cameras should cover the entire hotel; no space in the hotel should be surveillance-free."

Bindu: "OK, Sir."

"Good."

"Sir, I know a Pundit; shall we call him tomorrow?"

Jaswant Kumar: "Why?"

"The hotel has to be named formally; I mean, a Pundit should check the perfect moment, the right celestial conjunction, and give this place an auspicious name after doing a proper ceremony."

Jaswant Kumar: "Well, well, I don't believe in all this; as far as I am concerned, the naming has already been done."

Bindu: "Who named it?"

Jaswant Kumar: "Remember that day you called it amazing and unbelievable? Heaven spread over 7 acres; our hotel will be like this. Biggest and strongest that a storm cannot sway. The Titan Hotel. The name of our hotel will be The Titan Hotel (period)."

Date – 17/05/2011

Location: 17+69, 34+42, 04+23

Time: 5:00 (Evening)

Some technicians are putting up LED light boards on the roof of the hotel, spelling out the hotel's name in red and blue so that it is visible from almost a kilometers away, lending the place a spectacular and magical aura.

Jaswant Kumar and Bindu are watching from down below.

Bindu: "Finally, Sir, we showed the world what we are capable of."

Jaswant Kumar: "This evening will be the biggest and most memorable evening of my life. The dream that I had seen for years will finally come true. Titan is shining brightly in the sky. A new history is about to be created."

Jaswant whispers, "I can't explain in words how proud I feel!"

Bindu: "Now, what to do next, Sir?"

Jaswant Kumar: "So now we have to begin a search for bright minds who can take The Titan Hotel to the next level. It's time to get the best staff and managers in the country on board, a team that will give this hotel its identity- Let the hunt begin."

Just as the electronic signage comes to life, a flying crow collides with it and falls right at the foot of Jaswant Kumar. It has been electrocuted. The crow is not dead yet, but it is dying a painful death a few inches from Jaswant's feet… Jaswant suddenly feels uneasy. Can this be an ominous sign? A bad omen? A sign that something terrible is going to happen?

Chapter 4

The Hunt

Date: 04/07/2011

A month before now: In the dark of night, a car moves quietly. Inside, it's a scary sight - the floor is soaked in a lot of dark blood. Blood is dripping slowly from the seats. The inside of the car smells strongly of blood. Every time the car turned, the blood on the floor moved around.

Current Date: 03/06/2011

Location: 7B, Shastri Nagar, Jaisalmer

Time: 8:00 AM

Jaswant Kumar: "Can't you understand what I am trying to say?"

Kaishav Jain: "Come on, do I look like a small kid to you? But right now, you sound like one to me; you wish to hire just 6 staff for the entire hotel?"

Jaswant Kumar: "Well, it's not like that."

Kaishav Jain: "What is it like then? Please explain, because as far as I know, people here run a government Toilet facility with 6 staff... but a hotel like this? It sounds crazy."

"Right now, I don't have enough budget to fill the entire hotel with staff. I want to take a few months before I formally start running this hotel full house. So, I want to hire some well-qualified staff and see how things go from there; of course, I will be hiring more staff in a matter of time." Jaswant Kumar explains.

Kaishav Jain: "Ah! Now I get it. Smart! You are adapting the strategy of Real Jain Estate, less staff, more productivity."

Jaswant raises his hand to stop Kaishav ... "I know how Real Jain Estate operates... Now you understand my requirements. There should be 2 receptionists, both female, young and attractive, 2 staff for housekeeping and general maintenance, a top-quality chef, and a gatekeeper."

"Ok, give me a week," Kaishav Jain confirms.

Jaswant Kumar: "Kaishav, take note of one thing carefully. I want the staff to be professional, well-trained, helpful, humble, smart, and efficient. In other words, best of the best!

"Come on, Mr Kumar, I have stayed in many five-star hotels," Kaishav Jain interrupts Jaswant ... "I know what kind of people you need. Don't worry; I will get you the best staff for your hotel."

Date: 07/06/2011

Location: 7B, Shastri Nagar, Jaisalmer

Time: 9:30 (Morning)

"I am on my way to work," Jaswant Kumar informs Vaishali as he ties his shoelace.

"You didn't even have your breakfast properly. Why are you going so early?" Vaishali asks.

"Oh Yes, some customers are coming; I want to greet them personally," Jaswant says as he gets up to leave.

"What's the matter, Kumarji? You are getting busier every day," Vaishali asks as he picks up Jaswant's half-finished breakfast plate.

Jaswant Kumar: "Yes, almost 50% of the rooms are full since it opened."

Suddenly, a smile appeared on Vaishali's face. "Really? I am proud of you."

"Thanks, dear; now I must go. Oh yes, where is Mihir still sleeping?"

Vaishali Kumar: "No, no, he left for school before you woke up."

Jaswant Kumar walks up to his car, which is parked on the road right outside his house. Just as he tries to open the door, he hears someone call out his name, "Hey Jaswant ji…"

Jaswant Kumar turns around and spots the elderly lady staying right next door standing on the porch and waving to him. She is slightly bent due to old age, probably in her mid-eighties; as she smiles at Jaswant, a web of wrinkles fans out around her face. Her name is Phoolan Devi.

"How are you?" Jaswant Kumar asks the elderly lady.

"How will I be at this age? just about getting by. How are you?"

Jaswant Kumar: "We are all doing the same as you. Working away the days!"

"Tell me how your hotel is going." Devi asks.

Jaswant Kumar: "It is going very well, and that reminds me, I have to reach there now. See you later, Phoolanji. Bye for now!"

Phoolan Devi: "Yes, Kumar. You take care of yourself."

Location: The Titan Hotel

Time: 2:00 PM

Jaswant Kumar is sitting on a revolving chair in his office, talking on the phone: "Where are you? It's 2 o'clock in the afternoon?"

Kaishav Jain: "I am in my office. You know, at Real Jain Estate."

"Office? I am waiting for you from God knows when, and you are still at your office?" Jaswant asked, agitated.

Kaishav Jain: "No need to wait for me, Mr Kumar. Your staff van must be arriving any time now."

Jaswant Kumar: "And you? You are not coming?"

Kaishav Jain: " See, I have done what I was supposed to do; you don't need me now. And I have my own work to do…"

Jaswant Kumar hangs up the phone; he waits anxiously in his cozy office, wondering about the staff. The silence in this place is sometimes overwhelming. And then, the silence breaks with the sound of a vehicle pulling up in the driveway.

As he rushes toward the main entrance, Jaswant sees 6 people get out of a mini-van with their luggage.

"Welcome to The Titan Hotel." Jaswant Kumar rushes forward to greet the small party. "Come this way, please."

"There is a staff quarter with 20 rooms and a kitchen built right beside the main hotel building. This is going to be your residence from now; you are only 6, so you can pick and choose and stay where you please. I know all of you have come from far away, so settle down and freshen up; there is some food kept in the kitchen, so help yourself to it," Jaswant says as he guides the party of staff to the annex building.

"Once you are ready, come to the hotel lobby. My office is in the far-right corner. I will be working there."

Everyone selects their rooms and enters. Jaswant Kumar pays the mini-van driver, who then leaves with the vehicle. Sometime later, all 6 staff members arrive at the hotel lobby, where Jaswant is already waiting for them.

He instructs them to form a line. Following his request, they line up. Jaswant Kumar then directs each staff member to introduce themselves one by one, sharing their name, hometown, educational background, and work experience.

First up is Pushpa, a fair-complexioned, attractive lady.

"Sir, I am Pushpa; I am 24. I am from Indore and hold a Diploma in Hotel Management from Indore University. I have worked in the Balaji Hotel, and it is a very posh five-star establishment."

Great! Jaswant responds, and next…

Rinku is a medium-built young man in his mid-twenties.

Sir, I am Rinku, 23 years and so happy to be at this magnanimous hotel. I am a local from Jaisalmer and have worked at the Hyatt Hotel in Jaisalmer.

Reena is a 20-year-old, bespectacled woman. She is of medium height and build.

"Jaswant, Sir, I come from a small village in Bikaner. I am a commerce graduate from Banani Galsat College. Before coming here, I was working as a receptionist at Karni Bhavan Hotel in Bikaner."

Govardhan Singh is a heavy-set, mustachioed man of around 30.

Sir, I am from Jodhpur. I have been working as a gatekeeper for a very long time at Bhagirath Palace Hotel.

Bhopat is a 35-year-old male, medium-built and dark complexioned.

"Sir, I used to work in the kitchen of 'Vivanta Vadodara' in Gujrat. I am originally from Bihar, and my formal education is next to nothing, but I can give any five-star chef stiff competition. You name a dish, and I will make that in a jiffy. That's my challenge."

Jennifer is a slim, attractive, and beautiful 23-year-old girl. She is around 5 feet 5 inches in height.

"I am Jennifer; I hold a degree in Bachelor of Hotel Management. I was working as a room attendant in the Taj Hotel there."

Jaswant Kumar expresses his gratitude to the staff and then introduces himself.

"I was a businessman from Mumbai. A few years back, I started envisioning a dream, a dream of building a luxurious hotel in Jaisalmer's desert. Initially met with skepticism, this impossible dream has now turned into reality. The hotel's transformation from a camp of snakes and scorpions to a thriving establishment is a testament to my determination the belief in my vision."

"Today, this dream is going to move a step forward." Jaswant continues, "Why and how?"

Jaswant Kumar stretched both his hands, indicating the 6 people standing in front of him. "Here you are, a team of bright young men and women. I believe you will not hesitate to go that extra mile, work a little bit harder, and be ready to take risks to make this dream a reality. I want you guys to make my dream your own. People who do not have any goal in life and do not dream of moving forward are often stuck in one place. Success is achieved only by those who have a goal. I wish that the same goal should be yours, the same dream should be yours. The Titan Hotel is not only mine; it is ours from today. The future of this hotel depends on us. What you will do now is more important than what you did till today. We have to take Titan to such a level so that the vibration of our success reaches across the globe. And I will not be able to bring it alone. I need you all. I need your full dedication and trust. And I am sure if we work with honesty, determination, and solidarity, then no power in the world will be able to stop us from moving forward.

There are a total of 166 rooms in The Titan Hotel. Even if it is empty today, tomorrow it might be full of guests, and this is our aim. From today, we have to give all our hard work and devotion to Titan. We have to act now. So can I expect your full cooperation?"

"Yes, Sir," the staff replied in unison.

Jaswant Kumar: "Good. Now listen. Pushpa and Rina will look after the reception. Rinku will maintain the rooms, which he has been doing at his last job. Jennifer will look after maintenance and management. Govardhanji will be responsible for gatekeeping, and Bhopatji will take care of the kitchen."

Bhopat: "Don't worry, Sir, the food will be so good the guests will literally lick their fingers."

Jaswant Kumar: "When you are not working, please stay in your rooms. Don't go outside the hotel. If you need anything, you can come and tell me. Is that clear?"

"Yes, Sir," the staff responded together.

Jaswant Kumar: "OK, now all of you take a walk around the hotel, check-out the rooms and other amenities, go around slowly, and observe every detail."

The staff disperse and start touring the hotel. Pushpa and Reena enter a suite room together. Pushpa: "My

God!! This room is so big, with all the desired amenities, it's like a dream. Let's check-out the bed."

Pushpa jumps into the soft bed.

"No, no. We can't do that," Reena warns; "Remember, this is only for the guests. Sir has asked us to check everything. That means only checking, not using."

Pushpa: "What difference does it make? Come on; no one is watching; besides, we need to check the facilities first hand."

Reena: "No, this is wrong. Get up… get up; otherwise, you will spoil the bed."

Pushpa: "OK, I am getting up."

Pushpa gets up from the bed and tells Reena; that this is such a luxurious hotel; whoever stays here as a guest will have a lot of fun!

Date: 14/06/2011

Location: The Titan Hotel

Time: 11:30 (Morning)

Jaswant Kumar parks his car in front of the hotel and comes inside.

Jaswant Kumar: "Any progress?"

Pushpa: "No, Sir, not a single customer. Yes, but someone has come to meet you."

Jaswant Kumar: "Who?"

Pushpa: "He is sitting inside the storeroom."

Jaswant Kumar: "He is sitting in the storeroom? Why did you allow him there?"

Pushpa hesitated… "He insisted; he said he is your friend and didn't want to sit in the reception."

Reena: "Sir, here, take some water" She hands over a small bottle of water to Jaswant.

Jaswant Kumar: "Thanks, Reena." Pushpa, next time, don't just let anyone get into private spaces, no matter whatever they say, clear?"

Pushpa: "OK, Sir, I will keep that in mind.

★ ★ ★ ★

Jaswant Kumar goes to the storeroom and finds Bindu sitting on a chair, looking at his phone.

It's you, how come you wanted to wait here and not in the reception? Tell me, how are you today?"

Bindu: Sir, I like to talk to you in private and not in front of the staff; I am fine, Sir, but tell me, how is the business going?"

Jaswant Kumar: "No response so far; it's only been a few days now. You know, the hotel is not looking as grand as I envisioned it to be, maybe because of the part that is still incomplete. That's why I have cordoned off the area with under-construction signs and plastic sheets."

Bindu: "Sir, if you agree, I will get the remaining structure made?"

Jaswant Kumar: "How?"

Bindu: "I will talk to the builder; I can ensure that the job is done as soon as possible. You know, as soon as that section is done, the hotel will look complete. Sir, don't take tension; I will see what can be done. I am trying my best."

Date: 23/06/2011

Location: The Titan Hotel

Time: 10:00 PM

Jaswant Kumar has a broom in his hand; he is trying to clean a corner of the lobby.

Reena notices and rushes to be by his side. "What are you doing, Sir?"

Jaswant Kumar: "There were some spots on the floor; I am trying to clean it."

Reena: "Give it to me, Sir. What are we here for? Please, Sir, don't embarrass us."

Jaswant Kumar -"Thanks, but I am getting tired of sitting around!"

Reena takes the broom from his hand and says… "Sir, whatever you do, don't do this. This work is ours. But would you mind sharing what is worrying you so much?"

Jaswant Kumar: "Well, it's been close to one month, and still there is no customer. I am at a complete loss; I don't know what to do."

Reena: "Sir, it's only been a month, and you know, Sir, some things take time. And, Sir, this exclusive hotel you have built, it's no child's play to run a place like this. But one thing I want to tell you, and I am willing to vouch for it, one day, this hotel will become the most famous hotel in the whole world."

Jaswant Kumar: "Thanks, Reena. Thank you for the positive talk."

Jaswant is quiet for a while, reflecting on the situation, and then says, "I can't just sit around like this; I need to do something."

Date: 25/06/2011

Location: The Titan Hotel

Time: 9:00 AM

Jaswant is standing in the hotel lobby, and his staff are lined up in front of him. The men are wearing Mandarin collared coats, and the women are draped in elegant sarees with matching blue blazers. Jaswant had got the uniforms designed by a local designer and got the hotel logo embroidered on their uniforms.

Jaswant takes a deep breath and says… "When one move does not work, then one should move toward the next step. I believe the next step is advertising and networking. I will go out for a few days to market the hotel, and I want a member of the staff who can assist me and bring me success."

"Sir, Please let me come. I am passionate about this place, and I will be able to bring in customers…," Rinku says eagerly.

Jaswant Kumar puts up his hand to silence Rinku, "Listen, boy, I know you want to help, but this kind of networking will need something extra; it needs poise and experience, and who better to do this than Jennifer?"

"So, will you come, Jennifer?"

Date: 25/06/2011

Location: National Highway 114 (Jaisalmer – Jodhpur)

Time: 12:00 PM

Jaswant Kumar is driving the car, and Jennifer is sitting beside him in the passenger seat. She has changed into a pair of jeans and a black t-shirt but still carries the blue blazer to keep something of the uniform on when she visits the clients. A traditional Marwari song is playing on the radio…

"What a song! Wow. Although I do not listen to Marwari songs, this one is just amazing… Tell me, Jennifer, what kind of music do you like? Jaswant asks.

"Hip hop, rap etc etc…?"

"I don't listen to any type of music," Jennifer answers.

"Then you must be watching films? Any favorite actor?" Jaswant asks.

"I don't watch all this," Jennifer replies curtly.

"Well, do you have any hobbies?" Jaswant insists.

"No."

Jennifer takes out a cigarette from her pocket and searches her purse for a lighter.

"Oh, no, not in the car, please. I am allergic to smoke," Jaswant tells Jennifer.

Jennifer: "You should have thought before asking me to come with you."

A few minutes later, the car is parked at a petrol pump. The attendant is filling the tank. Jaswant Kumar has gone to a nearby store to get some snacks for the road. Jennifer gets out of the car and lights a cigarette.

The pump attendants stare at Jennifer; she is beautiful, and the fact that she is bold enough to smoke in a public place makes her even more attractive. But instead of looking away or feeling uncomfortable, Jennifer sternly stares back at the employees. After a while, Jennifer's stare makes them look away. That's when Jaswant arrives with the food.

Jaswant Kumar: "Not much option is there; I found this kachori. Here, take it."

Jennifer: "I don't eat all this, throw it away."

Location: High Top Hotel, Jodhpur Express

Time: 3:50 PM

Jaswant has gone inside the 'High Top Hotel' while Jennifer waits in the car.

Jaswant Kumar: "Hukum, I am a businessman, and my hotel, 'The Titan,' is just 100 kilometers off Jaisalmer. It is a luxury property with all amenities and is set amidst the grand dessert. It offers amazing views of the sand dunes while guests can enjoy all five-star amenities.

Hotel Owner: "But why are you telling me all this?"

Hukum, Jaswant continues, if any of your guests goes to visit Jaisalmer, please suggest my hotel's name. This is my card. If any guests come to my hotel through you, I promise you a commission of 10%.

Hotel Owner: "Brother, no guests tell when where they plan to go; they just move on their own accord."

Jaswant Kumar: "Hukum, I can see many foreigners are staying in your hotel; you can at least suggest to them my hotel's name."

"These English people don't trust us; they have more faith in their Google maps," the hotel owner laughs. "But still, I will try…"

Location: Bhagwati Hotel, Jodhpur

Time: 4:30 PM

Hotel owner: "Tell me where!!?"

Jaswant Kumar: "Around 100 km from Jaisalmer."

Hotel Owner: "That is close to the Pakistan Border, right? Sorry to say this, but only a dumb person will invest in a property there. You have opened your hotel in the middle of nowhere, and you expect people to go there and stay?"

Jaswant Kumar: "At least you can make an effort; after all, you have nothing to lose."

"No, brother, forgive me," the hotel owner refuses with folded hands.

Jaswant Kumar and Jennifer go to several hotels in Jodhpur, but they can't make any headway; everywhere, the response is negative.

Jennifer: "Now, what?"

Jaswant: "Next stop, Pushkar."

Date: 26/06/2011

Location: Lake View Hotel, Pushkar

Time: 1:00 PM

Hotel Owner: "Okay, you give your card. If someone goes that way, I will definitely send it."

Jaswant: "This is the card; the address is given on the back. Thank you. And if you ever come to Jaisalmer, do come."

Location: Shri Krishna Palace Hotel, Pushkar

Time: 2:30 PM

Hotel Owner: "Brother, the foreigners stay here for a couple of months. Why should I spoil my customer base by referring another hotel? Competition is stiff, and I don't see any logic behind promoting your hotel."

Date: 27/06/2011

Location: Padmavati Hotel, Jaipur

Time: 6:00 PM

Hotel Owner: "What did you say?"

Jaswant Kumar: "Yes, we offer a commission of 10% on each guest that comes from your reference. Will give you…"

Hotel Owner (cutting him off): "Do I look like a broker to you?"

Jaswant Kumar: "No, Hukum, by no means…

The hotel owner interrupts Jaswant: "…Please leave."

Location: Royal Palace Hotel, Jaipur

Time: 7:30 PM

Hotel Owner: "Yes, how many people are there?"

Jaswant Kumar: "No, no, I have not come to stay. I am a businessman. My hotel is 100 km ahead of Jaisalmer…"

The hotel owner turns his attention to his staff: "Listen, boy! It's time for check-out; go to room number 25."

Looking at Jaswant, he says, "Yes, go ahead…"

Jaswant Kumar: "If any of your guests goes to visit Jaisalmer…"

The hotel owner talks to his staff: "Where did Chanda go? It's time to clean all the empty rooms."

Now, turning to Jaswant: "Ok, I will think about it; you come to me sometimes if you happen to pass this path."

A car is parked outside the hotel in which Jennifer is sitting. Jaswant Kumar opens the car door and gets inside.

Jennifer: "What happened?"

Jaswant Kumar: "No use."

Jennifer: "Wait, let me do something; with that, she gets out of the car and enters the hotel.

Jennifer: "Hi, I was looking for the owner."

Hotel Owner: "Welcome, Madam. I am the owner. Are you looking for a room?"

Jennifer: "Your name, please?"

Hotel Owner: "Myself, Ramananda, Madam."

Jennifer smiles coyly and says, "Don't call me madam; it's Jennifer. Could you help me with some issues…?"

Hotel Owner: "Yes, why not? Please tell me."

Jennifer: "The man who came here a while ago, that man is my father, and as the daughter, I represent the owner of The Titan Hotel. I will be glad to do business with your firm. Would you be interested in finding out about our interest?"

After a while, Jennifer comes out of the hotel.

Jaswant Kumar: "What happened?"

Jennifer: "Done. He agreed to help."

"But how?" Jaswant Kumar asked, amazed.

"Well, well, there are some advantages of being a woman."

Date: 03/07/2011

Location: Joseph Property Construction Lines, Jaisalmer

Time: 8:00 PM

Don Robert is smoking a cigar in his office, and Bindu is sitting in front of him.

Bindu: "Sir, work has to start tomorrow itself."

Don Robert: "It won't be possible tomorrow; work will start after 3 days. I will have to make a new contract as well."

Bindu: "Okay."

Don Robert: "There will be a contract of 3.5 crores."

Bindu: "Yes, but at least give me a month, Sir. As I told you before, the party, I mean Jaswant Sir, is in a bad condition financially."

Don Robert: "Bad condition!! Hahaha! See, this deal is small, so I can't give that much time. Yeah, but I know the client pays on time, so I am making an exception. I will do the work, but the payment has to be on time."

Bindu: "Thank you, Sir.

Don Robert: "I will pass the contract today, don't worry, child."

Bindu comes out of the office and calls up Jaswant Kumar to share the happy news. But even after trying many times, the phone does not work.

Date: 04/07/2011

Location: 7B, Shastri Nagar, Jaisalmer

Time: 8:00 (Morning)

"Listen, I am leaving," Jaswant calls out to his wife.

"Why do you look so crestfallen today?"

"Why?" Jaswant asks, surprised. "No, I think it's your imagination."

"Looking at your face, I had that feeling. Are you feeling well?" Vaishali insists.

"Yes. Of course. What will happen to me?"

"How's work?" Vaishali asks. "The hotel is running smoothly?"

Jaswant Kumar: "It's going great, dear; we even have an advance booking."

Vaishali Kumar: "Oh, wow."

Location: The Titan Hotel Kitchen

11:00 AM

Jennifer: "What are you making?"

Bhopat: "Kadhi Chawal."

Jennifer: "Hmm, I guess till the guests start coming, we will have to do with simple food. Nothing special will be made; no use cooking lavish meals for the staff." Anyway, I have some maintenance work in the back side garden…"

Location: Reception, The Titan Hotel

Time: 11:30 AM

Pushpa and Reena are standing at the reception desk in their hotel uniforms.

"Have to enter the date in the register? Where is the register?" Reena bends down to check a drawer.

Pushpa: "What difference does it make? No one is coming. Take out the register, enter the date, and draw lines; that is the only work left for us to do."

Reena: "So what? It's our duty, and don't think so negatively. Maybe today a guest will turn up, maybe tomorrow there will be a whole group of people. Maybe I will get to write the name of the first guest in the register today… who knows when fate will smile at us?"

After some time, they hear a car honking in the driveway.

"Is it, Sir?" Pushpa asks.

"No, he is already at the hotel." Reena replies.

"Then whose car, is it? Rinku, will you go and check outside, please?" Pushpa asks Rinku.

Rinku opens the large glass door of the hotel entrance and steps outside to check, then he returns and says enthusiastically, "I think they are the first guests."

"Oh really?" Reena exclaims in excitement, "You know how to greet them right."

"Pushpa, fix your hair, and the register is in place? And Rinku, fix your tie."

Pushpa: "Yes, yes. Rinku, go and stand near the front door. As soon as the guest arrives, open the door with a welcoming gesture."

Rinku: "Yes, yes, I am all set."

Pushpa: "Ok. Everyone get ready."

The car halts right in front of the gate, and 3 men come out of the car. Govardhan Singh rushes to greet them.

Govardhan Singh: "Sir, any luggage?"

The men walk past him in silence.

Govardhan Singh holds open the door for them while Rinku is waiting at the other end of the door.

Rinku: "Welcome, Sir. Please let me take you to the reception."

Pushpa: "Good morning, Sir. Welcome to The Titan Hotel. How can I assist you?"

The men remain silent. They look around the place as if searching for something or someone.

Pushpa:"Sir, one room for the 3 of you, or do you want separate rooms?

We have rooms starting range from 6700 INR to 85000 INR per day. I will tell you what benefits you will get with the rooms; all rooms come with complimentary breakfasts. Sir, we can show the rooms or give a tour of the entire property. We provide restaurant facility, swimming pool, gym, camel ride, desert safari…"

Jaswant Kumar was watering a lawn when he heard loud voices inside. Is it the distinct sound of someone talking loudly, an argument? Then, there is no doubt that things are very wrong when he hears the glass crashing and metal banging against the floor!

Sensing something was very wrong, he left the hosepipe and rushed to the reception, but halfway through the lawns, he noticed 3 men coming from the direction of the hotel toward him.

Jaswant Kumar slows down and asks with a smile, "Hello, Sir; how can I help you?"

The men look at him in silence, and Jaswant has an odd feeling.

The pathway is lined with large earthenware pots, and one of the men bends down to pick up a pot. Before

Jaswant can react, he brings down the heavy pot with considerable force on Jaswant Kumar's head. Jaswant falls down from the impact, and his whole face is covered in deep, red blood, trickling down to his shirt… A half-formed scream escapes his throat, and then he falls unconscious. The men drag him to a storeroom and lock the door from inside.

Present

Time: 8:00 PM

Ramanuj: "Who were the men?"

Bindu: "What do I say, the cruel hands of fate? Whatever you have heard till now is only the tip of the iceberg. The real story is about to begin now. None of us had ever imagined in our wildest dreams what was about to happen next. A storm that we never expected to come, a destiny so bloody and gruesome that my heart shrinks thinking about it…"

Ramanuj: "At least tell me who is after all this? Whose men hit him with the pot?"

Bindu: "Kalu Singh."

Chapter 5

The First Guest

A Day Before the Present:

A black car is being washed in the garage. One worker has applied soapy lather to the car's body, while another diligently sprays it down with a hose. Strangely, the water streaming into the drain takes on an unsettling resemblance to blood. Dark blood mixed with bubbles drains into the gutter. Once the cleaning is finished, a member of the garage staff etches certain marks at the rear of the car using a knife.

Location: Storeroom of The Titan Hotel

Time: 12:00 PM

The silence in the storeroom is suffocating, magnifying even the slightest movement or sound. In the partially illuminated room and among rows of white linen stacked up in steel racks, Jaswant Kumar is lying on the blood-soaked carpeted floor in a semi-conscious state- the blood stains on his shirt have dried, and so has the wound on his head to some extent. 3 men are staring down at him. Aslam, dark and muscular, stands with his legs apart. Pappu is a big man; the white button-down shirt he is wearing barely conceals his ripping muscles, and Kalu Singh, a tall man, emits an aura of raw power.

"He has made a grave mistake; he has provoked me, and the mere sight of him makes my blood boil with rage," Kalu Singh says, looking down at Jaswant Kumar. "I feel like tearing his muscles right now!"

They stand in silence for some time, and then Kalu Singh bursts into a heart-wrenching laughter that echoes through the room. "I can't believe this meek-looking bastard had the balls to do all this, he says, looking at Aslam." Now he nudges Jaswant with the tip of his shoes… "Hey, you listen, you have only 2 days; all this should be transferred to my name. Understood? Just 2 days."

Kalu Singh and his men walk out of the storeroom. Jaswant Kumar is still lying on the floor, his limbs gripped by raw fear. Never in his wildest dream had he thought that suddenly, everything would change so much.

Out of nowhere, a loud gunshot pierces through the eerie silence of the room; through the horrifying atmosphere, The air fills with terrified screams echoing all around. Jaswant, paralyzed with fear, suddenly jolts to his feet, his eyes wide with terror. For a few minutes, he regains his balance and limps his way toward the reception area from where the sound seems to have originated. Jaswant Kumar cannot believe the scene in front of him. Is it part of some bizarre dream? He has to lean against a pillar in the lobby to keep himself from falling.

Blood is splattered everywhere on the carpet. Reena is lying on the floor, bleeding from the neck, where apparently, she has been shot. Pushpa is also lying on the floor, but she doesn't have any visible injury. Govardhan Singh is checking Pushpa's pulse. Bhopat is standing transfixed, watching in sheer bewilderment.

"Sir, we tried a lot to stop them from going inside, but they started vandalizing. They came back and fired. Didn't know how to stop them," Rinku explains.

While Jaswant is looking at the scene and trying to make sense of everything, Bhopat suddenly gets up and starts running toward the gate. Sensing trouble, Jaswant Kumar follows him. Bhopat opens the hotel gate and rushes out into the driveway.

"What the hell are you doing?" Jaswant Kumar asks as he catches up with him with some effort.

"I am leaving; what else do you expect me to do? Risk my life for this job?" Bhopat asks, trembling. "I don't want to die."

Jaswant Kumar: "Look, calm down; you are not going anywhere; please understand."

"What was all that?: He says, pointing inside the hotel. "She was shot right in front of my eyes, and I can be next… I have a wife and children back home…"

"If you step out and try to run, you will be killed. Trust me, here you will be safe," Jaswant tries to convince him.

As Jaswant is trying to convince Bhopat, Govardhan Singh calls out to him in an urgent voice. "We are losing time here. Reena is bleeding, and you need to come inside right now."

"Look, nothing will happen to you. Not only you, but nothing will happen to anyone. Forget what has happened, and let's go inside. If by mistake you peep outside, they will kill you. The Titan Hotel is a safe place for now, but stepping outside is not. Please understand my point," Jaswant says, holding Bhopat's hand before guiding him inside the hotel.

Location: Jaisalmer – Munabao Road

Time: 1:30 PM

"Bloody rascals act as if they own the road," Bindu murmurs under his breath. He saves himself from falling as a black Scorpion brushes past him at break-neck speed. Bindu pauses for a minute, catching his breath and balance, and then resumes his ride to The Titan Hotel through the desert road.

Back at the hotel lobby, Jeniffer is holding a kitchen towel to Reena's neck, trying to arrest the blood flow. Rinku is sprinkling water on Pushpa's face. Bhopat is standing, soaking in the scene. The feeling of excitement as the 3 men walked in through the door, presumably as the first guests less than an hour ago, has turned into a nightmare, and now a horrid silence is suspended in the lobby.

"You can't just stand there and do nothing, Govardhan shouts at Jaswant. "She is dying, can't you see?"

"She is bleeding profusely; we have to go to the hospital immediately," Jennifer adds.

Jaswant Singh – "Breathing?"

Jennifer: "Yes."

Jaswant Kumar: "And Pushpa?"

"She is unconscious from shock, nothing else. Now, can we please make an effort and go to the hospital?" Govardhan Singh says in agitation.

"You bring Reena out; I will bring the car right in front of the gate," Jaswant Kumar says, looking at Jennifer and Govardhan. "He then turns to the rest of the staff and says in a stern voice, "No one leaves the hotel until I come back. Remember, this is for your own safety."

Govardhan and Jennifer make Reena lie down in the back seat of the car.

"I am also coming," Jennifer declares and gets in the car, tenderly positioning Reena's head on her lap.

As Jaswant starts the car, Bindu's bike zooms into the hotel premises. Bindu parks his bike and waves at Jaswant's car. "Please stop, Sir, please!"

Jaswant had no other choice but to pull up; Bindu opened the front door and hopped into the passenger seat. Without saying a word, Jaswant starts driving.

"Sir, where have you been? Bindu asks, fastening his seat belt. "I have been trying to call you since morning.

I have got some good news. Don Robert has agreed to complete our remaining project."

"You shouldn't have been here now, Bindu." Jaswant Kumar says quietly, knitting his eyebrows and looking straight ahead.

Jennifer suddenly speaks up, "Who were those people?"

Bindu: "Which people? What are you talking about?"

"I need to know who they were?" Jennifer repeats

"They were goons, Kalu Singh and his men," Jaswant answers.

Bindu: "What?"

Bindu turns to look at Jennifer, and then he realizes it is not just Jennifer sitting in the back seat; a bloodied Reena is lying on her lap.

"Oh, my God!" Bindu says, almost jumping out of his seat, shocked beyond belief. "When did this happen? What is going on?"

"She is losing blood every minute. Can you please hurry up?" Jennifer speaks with urgency.

Bindu turns to Jaswant and asks, "Please tell me what is happening. Sir?

"Bindu, there is no time to explain things now…"

Bindu is literally shaking, "I can see that the girl has been shot; I deserve to know."

Jaswant Kumar (shouting): "Could you please be quiet and let me drive? This is not the time to answer your questions."

Bindu: "I'm sitting in a car where a girl is bleeding, and you don't want me to ask questions. Wait, I need to inform the police."

Jaswant Kumar: "No, don't do that. I am telling you, I am… Well, it's a complicated matter. The land on which this hotel stands, the land I had bought legally from the government… now Kalu Singh claims it as his own. He was in illegal possession of this land… and this morning he walked into the hotel with 2 goons and did this…"

"Whaaatt?" Bindu interrupts… "If you knew that this land was in the possession of that goon. Then why did you take it?"

"I didn't know, Bindu, I didn't know," Jaswant says, nodding his head from side to side in exasperation. "It all happened suddenly. He came into the hotel posing as a guest, threatened, vandalized, shot the girl, and left. He was serving a life sentence in jail. I had no idea that he would get bail, but he did."

The towel that Jenifer had wrapped around Reena's neck is soaked in blood; observing this, Bindu takes off his jacket and gives it to Jennifer. "Try to press it to the neck." Then he turned to Jaswant and said, "Sir, first we will go to the hospital, and then we will report this to the police."

"No, no, no! Can you imagine what hell will break loose if we do that? Before anything happens, we will be killed. You don't know Kalu Singh. If he comes to know that we have gone to the police station, everything will be over even before the police can react."

"If we don't go, then we will be trapped; the whole blame will fall on us. We have proof. Everything is captured on CCTV," Bindu insists.

"You don't understand." Jaswant says, his voice tinged with distress, "He is a predator. Don't even think of confronting him if you want to stay alive."

"Then what do you propose to do now?"

"Give me time to think," Jaswant says, looking ahead.

While pressing the accelerator, Jaswant notices that the blood has trickled down to his feet. Reena is getting worse. As he drives along the almost deserted road, he tries to focus; this is not going to be easy. He sees a dirt road going into the desert and then takes a sharp turn.

"Where are you going?" Bindu shrinks. "The road to Jaisalmer is straight ahead."

"This is a shortcut," Jaswant Kumar says, looking straight ahead.

Reena is going in and out of consciousness; her eyes are half-closed, and her voice has become a faint murmur. Jennifer looks helplessly at Reena and bends down to hear Reena whisper in a barely audible voice… "I don't want to die…, please save me."

Jennifer runs her fingers through Reena's hair, "Nothing will happen to you. Just try to relax; we are on our way to the hospital."

The car bumps and rolls through the dirt road, and suddenly, a military check post looms into view.

"My God, Look at that!" Bindu exclaims, "There is a checkpoint up ahead; we are screwed now; we are gone. Take a U-turn! Right now."

Jaswant Kumar: "We can't."

Bindu: "Are you in the right place of your mind? We're gonna get caught… I said, take a U-turn."

Jaswant Kumar (irritated): "I can't. They have already seen us, and if we turn now, they will be suspicious…" Jaswant shouts at Bindu in anger, "For God's sake, Bindu, don't panic. And don't get out of the car at any cost," Jaswant Kumar instructs.

"No, I will not do this; I won't be privy to your lies…" Bindu says defiantly.

"If you wish to see Reena alive, do as I say," Jaswant says through clenched teeth.

The car reaches a BSF post, and a soldier flags down the car. The soldier bent down to look through the window at Jaswant and asked, "What's up, brother? Where are you going?"

"Going to Jaisalmer, Hukum."

"Jaisalmer? By this road? The soldier asks suspiciously. "Why don't you step out of the car."

Jaswant says, "Hukum, it's an emergency; I need to go there as quickly as possible."

"Then… Come out quickly and show me the car papers…" the soldier commands.

Jaswant Kumar opens the door and reluctantly steps out of the car, then he bends down again to look for the car papers inside the car… the soldier notices the fresh wound on Jaswant's head.

"Wow, that is an interesting wound. It's still fresh and bleeding. Did you have a wild adventure or a wrestling match?" He asks, mocking.

A second soldier joins the first soldier; "What is happening? Who is this man?"

Before Jaswant or the first soldier gets a chance to answer, the second soldier says, "Look, there are blood stains on the car, he raises his rifle to aim at Jaswant. Get the car checked right now," he barks.

The first soldier checks the papers and asks Jaswant to open the car trunk… The back windows are rolled up, and Jennifer has cleverly covered up Reena with a shawl she was carrying. Inside the car, Bindu sits paralyzed in fear.

The second peeps inside the car, trying to look through the tinted glass… "Who is inside? Ask them to step out now." he orders Jaswant.

"Hukum, listen to me; it will be a great favor if you let us go. My daughter-in-law is in the car; she got a woman's disease… er… vaginal infection. She is bleeding heavily, and the only way to save her is to take her to the hospital as soon as possible; she is not even in a position to sit up. The girl is her sister. If you don't get to the doctor soon, then my daughter-in-law's life will be in danger."

Jaswant now folds his hands and says, "Have mercy, Sir. A few months back, she had a miscarriage, and now this," he says in desperation. "It's her life in question."

The first soldier looks at the backseat through the tinted glass and makes out a woman sitting and another woman lying on her lap.

"Which village are you from?"

Jaswant replies, "Moti Ki Berry, Hukum."

"Are you aware where you were heading? Don't you know this location and the potential dangers associated with it? If you continue on this path, you will enter the Red Zone, which is near the Pakistan Border. Once you get caught there, the consequences will be severe – no one will check or inquire like we are doing; they will straight away shoot all of you. For your safety, I strongly urge you to turn back immediately. Look out for the upcoming intersection and take a right onto the main road, which will guide you to Jaisalmer without any risk." The first soldier explains.

The second soldier lowers his rifle, saying, "Sir, I believe it would be prudent to investigate this situation further, as it appears the situation, the wound, and the blood stains are suspicious. This is definitely not normal."

"Naah… Just let them go. It's an emergency situation. It doesn't seem suspicious to me. We should release them quickly since they don't have much time left." the first soldier says.

"Thank you, Hukum," Jaswant responds with folded hands. "I am very grateful."

"Now, move quickly from here if you want to save her," the first soldier tells him rudely before walking off to his post.

Once inside the car and out of the vision of the post guards, Jaswant lets out a sigh of relief.

"That was close," Bindu says, "but still, we need to hurry."

Jaswant drives through the same desert road in silence, "Jaisalmer is still 70 kilometers from here he says after a while, "and it will take at least 4 hours to reach there even if I try my best."

Jaswant drives the car into a desolate area leading to the ruined remains of an old Haveli that had stood there centuries ago.

"Oh no! Not again! What is going on with your mind? Why do you keep missing the road?" Bindu says, visibly agitated.

"Now, there is no other way…"

Bindu: "What do you mean?"

Jaswant Kumar: "The body will have to be burned."

"Have you gone insane? Do you know what you are talking about…" Bindu shouts at Jaswant in shock.

"There is no chance to save her; she is almost dead; even if there were a little chance of survival, I would have tried, but no, there isn't, and you know it. 4 hours have passed since the bullet entered her body…"

"No, I don't agree with you. How can you give up like this? We will go to Jaisalmer. There are still chances," Bindu argues.

Jaswant Kumar: "Even if we take her to Jaisalmer, she will not survive."

"How can you do this? You can't just dispose of her like this, can you?" Bindu asks, shocked.

Jaswant Kumar: "Okay, let's assume we go to Jaisalmer. She will be declared dead, and there will be a procedure and autopsy, and the report will be handed to the police. The police will lodge a case, an investigation will be done. Then what? We will be under suspicion for one, and then Kalu Singh's name will come. We will have to face Kalu Singh and his henchmen and the police interrogation. The price will be heavy."

Bindu: "I can go through all that but getting rid of a girl like this. It's insane. No, I am not playing this game. Sorry, I refuse to be a part of this. And if u have any humanity left, don't dare to do this."

"… It may also backfire… Kalu Singh wields a lot of power." Jaswant continues. "He can do whatever he wants; he can kill us or get us behind bars. As for Reena, I can say with certainty that she won't live; looking at her face, I can say that she has already passed away."

Jaswant Kumar parks the car close to the ruins. Once upon a time, it had been a massive structure, a Royal family's house maybe, but now all that remains of it are some stumps, pillars, and a few broken arches oddly dinging mid-air and one or 2 portions of the wall, worn down by the hands of time. Shrubs have grown through the cracks in the cement, and here and there, garbage is strewn, beer cans, and broken glass from liquor bottles, proclaiming the fact the place is used now and then for all the wrong reasons.

Bindu opens the door and walks off in anger.

Jaswant Kumar: "Jennifer, please help me move the body."

"I am not going to be a part of this…" Jennifer says with a stoic expression.

Jaswant Kumar gently lifts Reena from the backseat and carries her to the center of the ruins with some effort. Then he pauses for a few minutes, probably catching his breath before uprooting the shrubs lying here and there and breaking the branch of a dried-up tree that stands alone at the back of the ruins—almost half an hour passes before he spreads them all over Reena's body.

Jaswant walks up to the car, takes out a petrol drum, and rolls it toward the site. He then pours petrol on the body. Jennifer has gotten out of the car now and is leaning on the side of it, smoking a cigarette. Jaswant Kumar walks up to her and asks for her lighter. "I don't have," Jennifer says, looking away.

"Please, Jennifer," Jaswant pleads. "Don't make it more difficult for me."

Jennifer reluctantly takes out the lighter from her pocket and hands it over to him.

Slowly, the fire catches, and shrubs and the wiry branches crackle. Within a few moments, the flame grows, leaping with the force of a demon engulfing the slight body of Reena, the young and exuberant girl who had been full of life only this morning. Jaswant Kumar notices, to his horror, Reena's fingers moving before the flames swallow them and turn them into jelly. The wind is strong. From a distance, Jennifer can smell flesh as a gust of wind blows into her face, and from far away, Bindu notices the embers of fire going toward the sky from a distance. Thick, dark smoke spreads everywhere. Darkness engulfs the skyline like a curse. The place that was calm before now looks strange and frightening, like something out of a scary… It feels like fear is hanging in the air.

The 3 sit in silence as they drive toward the hotel.

"Listen, we have to say that Reena was taken to Jaisalmer Hospital, and she was kept in the ICU; now she is out of danger. The doctor has said that Reena will have to stay there for a few days to recover."

"Why did you keep the petrol drum in the trunk of your car?" Jennifer asks.

"Because my hotel is 100 kilometers away from Jaisalmer and there is no petrol pump on the way, and as I travel every day, I keep it as a standby in case I run out of fuel. I had kept the drum for safety. Why do you both seem to be doubting me? Trust me, what I did was for our good, and there was no other way out."

Just then, Jaswant Kumar's phone rings.

"Hello, Where are you?" Vaishali asks in an agitated voice.

"What happened?"

"When can you come?"Vaishali replies.

"Vaishali? Tell me what happened… Vaishali? Hello? Hello? Are you there?"The phone gets disconnected.

Jaswant Kumar immediately dialed Vaishali's number, but he got the beeping sound. The phone doesn't connect.

Location: The Titan Hotel

Time: 6:30 PM

The car screeches to a halt in front of the hotel. As soon as they get off, everyone rushes outside, eager for news of Reena.

Pushpa: "What happened? How is Reena?"

"Oh, Thank God you are up on your feet," Jaswant says, looking at Pushpa. "About Reena, there is nothing to worry about. She is being treated, and she will be absolutely fine. Right now, she is admitted, but I assure you she will join us in a few days."

Govardhan Singh: "Who was he? The man who did all this?"

"I will tell you everything tomorrow. Now, listen carefully. You all have to stay at the hotel tonight, pick any room, and make yourself comfortable," Jaswant Kumar says in an urgent tone, "Govardhan…"

"Yes?"

"Lock the main gate from outside and lock the hotel door from inside; no one should go out or come into the hotel while I am back. Got it?" Jaswant instructs.

"Sir, do you think he might come back?" Pushpa asks.

"No, no. There is nothing to panic. And no, they will not come back, but your safety is my first priority. I don't want to take any risks. Do you all understand?" Jaswant clarifies.

"But Sir…" Pushpa is silenced by Jaswant… "All your questions will be answered tomorrow. I promise. Now I have to go for some important work…"

"Take care that no one goes out of the hotel."

"Wait, Sir, you went to Jaisalmer and came back within 6 hours. Is it possible? And that too after getting Reena admitted to the hospital?" Govardhan Singh asks suspiciously.

"Yes, we went at high speed, and I knew a shortcut that saved us a lot of time. Thank God the hospital took immediate action and started treating Reena."

"Which shortcut?" Govardhan Singh asks, frowning.

"Listen, I will give you all the details tomorrow. We will have the discussion you want, but now I have to go," Jaswant says.

Jaswant Kumar walks up to Jennifer, lowers his voice to a whisper, and says… "Please don't tell anyone what happened."

Jaswant spots Bindu sitting on his bike in silence. "Bindu, come with me," Jaswant tells him as he gets to his car.

"I am not going to come with you," Bindu says as he starts his bike.

"It is late; it is risky to go on the bike alone, and because of what happened today, going anywhere alone can be risky."

"I still can't believe what happened today and what you did," Bindu says with disdain.

"I can understand your feelings, but the safest thing for you to do right now is to come with me. That's the best option for you. So, please understand what I am saying: leave the bike here and come with me." Jaswant.

Location: Munabao - Jaisalmer Road

Time: 8:00 PM

Jaswant wants to get home as soon as possible. The call from Vaishali has left him worried, and the fact that he couldn't get through to her has added to his woes.

"Can you please drive a little slowly?" Bindu says as Jaswant zips through the road.

Jaswant Kumar's phone rings at that precise moment.

It's Vaishali. "Where are you?

"I have been trying to call you; why do you sound like this?" Jaswant asks.

"Listen, 3 people are standing in front of the house for the last 2 hours. I was peeping through the window, and one of them stared at me."

"Vaishali, where is Mihir?" Jaswant is now at his wit's end.

"He… he is…"Vaishali stammers, unsure what to say.

"Where is Mihir?" Jaswant repeats, almost screaming into the phone.

"He has gone to Phoolan Devi's house? Why? What happened? Who are these men? Is there a problem, Jaswant?"Vaishali asks.

"Listen to me carefully; go to Mihir right now."

"Will you tell me what happened?"Vaishali shouts back.

"This is not the time to answer questions. Go to Mihir as soon as possible and go through the back door. Those people should not see you. Make sure you wear something or cover yourself up so that they can't make out even if they spot you from a distance. Please, Vaishali, don't waste time. Do it now," Jaswant instructs.

"Yes, Yes, I am going…"

"And be on call, don't disconnect," Jaswant says.

Vaishali walks out of the back door of the house. She then quietly knocks on Phoolan Devi's door.

"Oh! Come in, Vaishali. Why are you covering your head like that?"

"Where is Mihir?" Vaishali asks without answering her.

Phoolan Devi: "He was just playing with Ranu. They are in the back garden. What happened, dear? Why do you look so nervous?"

Vaishali Kumar runs to the garden where Mihir and Ranu are playing.

"Mihir is in front of me," Vaishali tells Jaswant on the phone.

Jaswant breathes a sign of relief. "Now, hear me out carefully. Take Mihir, take the back road, and go as far away from the house as possible. I don't care if you get on a rikshaw, a taxi, or anything; just go to some busy place in the city and, check in to a hotel and then text me the address. Settle into a room, and I will come and join you soon. I am coming."

"And the house? Are you saying I should just leave it? Just like that and go? What about all the things, the clothes, my jewelry… important documents? No, absolutely not!"

Vaishali shouts at Jaswant.

"I swear to you, don't go home. Your life is in danger," Jaswant cries into the phone. "Jaswant, what have you done?" Vaishali asks, her voice choking with emotion.

"I will tell you everything once we meet. Now please do as I am telling you to… Quick. You don't have time, so act now. There is no time to talk," Jaswant says, finding it hard to concentrate on the road ahead.

Vaishali Kumar hangs up.

"Mummy, see, Ranu is not letting me play with his garden set," Mihir says. Without answering, Vaishali picks up Mihir and walks toward the back road.

"What happened, Ma? Where are we going?" Mihir asks, surprised at his mother's action.

As Vaishali comes through the back garden and into a narrow lane, she spots a taxi waiting at the end of the lane.

She knocks on the glass window and asks, "Bhaiya, will you take me to Pansari Bazaar?"

As mother and son settle in the backseat, and Vaishali pulls up the black dupatta she has wrapped around her head, the taxi takes a turn to move past their house…

Vaishali's blood freezes as she notices the 3 men breaking the door of their house with iron rods.

Location: Munabao – Jaisalmer Road

Time: 9:00 PM

Jaswant perspires despite the car's strong air-conditioning. He clutches the steering wheel, even as his whole body is shaking with anxiety.

"What is happening? Why did you ask them to leave the house?"

Jaswant Kumar does not answer; he is clutching the steering wheel and looking straight ahead.

Bindu "Mister Kumar. I am asking what happened."

Jaswant Kumar: "Yes?"

Bindu throws up his hands in the air, "What's going on? Will you say something?"

"We are heading toward disaster! Absolute disaster. That's what is happening!"

Chapter 6

The Plan

(2 days from the present):

Hungry flames, yellow and orange, shot up high, turning the sky black with smoke. The factory was burning down, with its buildings falling apart like a house of cards. Firefighters were there with big hoses, working hard to put out the big flames. Police were busy looking for clues and keeping the crowd under control. TV reporters were also there, going through the dirty water and smoke to report on what was happening.

Location: Empire Hotel, Jaisalmer

Time: 12:30 AM

Receptionist: "How can I help you, Sir?"

"Ma'am, my wife is staying in room number 86," Jaswant says, fidgeting with his ring.

"Your name, please?" the lady asks, staring at her desk screen.

"Jaswant Kumar."

"Just a moment, Sir," the lady answered in a practiced voice and picked up the receiver.

"Ma'am, someone named Jaswant Kumar is here to see you… she listens for a moment," hangs up, and says in a more relaxed voice… "Sir, you can go upstairs or take the lift; room number 86 is on the right as you take the corridor."

Vaishali opens the door just a crack to ensure who is on the other side. Then, opens it wider to let him in… "Where have you been?"

"Where is Mihir?" Jaswant asks as he storms into the room.

Vaishali Kumar sits on the bed without answering. Mihir is sleeping on the bed.

"Did anyone see you coming here, I mean, those people?" Jaswant grills Vaishali.

"What the hell is happening? Who were those people? And how did you get this injury on your head? what's going on?" Vaishali asks angrily.

Jaswant heaves a sigh, nods his head, and says, "It was just an insignificant accident that blew out of proportion."

"An insignificant accident. Are you kidding me? You asked me to leave the house, our house, and every damn thing we owned in there. Those people were breaking into the house while I was leaving in the car… and…"

"Wait, what? They were breaking into the house, hitting the door?" Jaswant Kumar

"Jaswant, tell me what happened. Tell me the truth."

"Okay, let me explain. Whatever is happening, it's not my fault. Yesterday, I got out of home as usual, and while passing by Bhati Circle, suddenly, a car came from the opposite direction at break-neck speed. I somehow averted a collision, thank God! Although I could avoid the accident, the cars scratched against each other. Obviously, I felt wronged. I asked the person driving the car to compensate for the damage. But instead, he started quarreling and hurling abuses at me. I lost my temper, but you know I am not up to those tacky fights. So, I went to the police station and lodged an FIR.

Later, I realized these people were not easy to deal with; they were vindictive. I thought they might look up my address and come to the house to settle the score, and they did exactly that…"

"Really, so this is all about road rage? So, did you find out what happened? They entered our house just like that? What if they come back and try to harm me or our child?" Vaishali asked incredulously. "We should complain to the police about this."

"No, no, it will be risky. Do you see this injury on my head? This is a reason to fight those people. Those people are locals; they are antisocial. I found out about it much later when I had already lodged the complaint. I don't want this matter to go further."

"So, what now?"

"Give me time to think."

"Don't forget that whatever we have, it's here. We have nothing else."

"I am tired of whatever happened today. Maybe we should sleep. Did you have dinner?" Jaswant asked, ignoring Vaishali's plea.

"I am wondering, why is there always trouble with you? How long will all this last?" Vaishali says, almost tearful now.

"Relax, Vaishali, everything will be fine. We will talk tomorrow."

As the 3 of them sleep peacefully, Jaswant's phone starts to vibrate. It is 2 am, Jaswant silently gets up, moves to the balcony, and says… "What happened?"

"The work is done. The car is as if it has just come from the showroom." Kaishav Jain says on the other side of the phone.

"The blood…?" Jaswant whispers.

"Everything has been cleaned and washed, and the scratches should be visible. Yes, it was a little difficult to make it look authentic, but you know, I can get anything done. Tomorrow morning the car will be in front of the Empire Hotel. The work was extremely risky. If it were someone else, he would have charged 30%, but since we have been together for some time now, I will charge only 20%. Earlier payment is also due; in case you have forgotten, you know my policy, right?" Kaishav Jain said, lowering his voice.

"Can we talk tomorrow?" Jaswant said and hung up.

Location: Empire Hotel, Jaisalmer

Time: 9:30 (Next Day, Morning)

"I am leaving. Remember, don't go out of the hotel until I come back. If you want anything, call the reception and order whatever you like; if Mihir wants to drink juice, let him have it; don't be too hard on him. And take care, dear." Jaswant said as he got up to leave.

"Swear on me, you will not do anything that will harm us. Before doing anything, think about your son…"

"I am not going to do anything of that sort, Vaishali. I am going to resolve the matter. I will try to convince them. If needed, I will apologize. But I will end this matter and come back. I know everything, Vaishali; you both are my life. Nothing bad will happen to us; I know you are worried but have faith. This may look like a difficult time, but it will pass." Jaswant says, clasping Vaishali's hands in his.

Location: Government Registration Office, Jaisalmer

Time: 10:00 (Morning)

Jaswant Kumar parks the car in front of the office and rushes inside the office. "Hey, wait, where are you going like this?" the lady at the reception interrupts Jaswant.

"Madam, this is urgent; please let me go inside."

"Sir has just come in; let me check with him first," the lady says sternly. "Meanwhile, you wait there."

Just then, Chhagan Singh called from inside, "Let him come in…"

Jaswant Kumar enters the office, the same office he had walked into almost 2 years before to sign the final contract to purchase the land. But today, he is agitated, at his wit's end.

Chhagan Singh looks up from his chair; a pile of files is scattered on the table in front of him.

"Sir, I want to sell my land and hotel. Today, right now!" Jaswant Kumar says in a loud voice.

"Hmmmm… You want to sell the land?" Chhagan Singh asks in a bland voice.

"Yes, and the hotel along with it."

"Yes, understood. But there should also be a buyer for it," Chhagan Singh says. "Kalu Singh, everything needs to be transferred in his name and today itself." Jaswant Kumar says.

Chhagan Singh: "OK, I get it. But I will need Kalu Singh's documents to process everything."

" I will get it, as soon as possible."

"Okay then, till then, fill the form outside and submit it. Chhagan Singh hands him a form."

"I am in urgent; please put it in the procedure today itself."

"Hmmmm… the procedure will be done. You just get the documents."

As Jaswant Kumar starts to leave, Chhagan Singh calls out after him, "I hope that whatever steps you take from now on, you will have your family's best interest in mind."

Location: The Titan Hotel

Time: 12:30 (Noon)

Jaswant Kumar screeches to a halt in front of the hotel. Goverdhan Singh opens the gate and rushes out to check. He takes the keys from Jaswant and parks the car.

They enter the lobby together, where everyone is sitting idly.

"How is everyone?" Jaswant asks in a cheerful voice.

"Sir, a call came from Reena's family," Pushpa says, getting up from the sofa.

"On whose phone?" Jaswant asks, knitting his eyebrows.

"The phone at the reception desk."

Really?" Jaswant asks, puzzled.

"It was Reena's father, Sir; he wanted to talk to Reena; he said he hadn't reached her on the phone since yesterday."

Jaswant Kumar: "What did you say?"

"Sir, I hung up the phone. I didn't know what to say; I thought I should ask you before answering," Pushpa said nervously.

"Do you have his father's number?"

"No, Sir."

"Okay."

"Sir, how is Reena now? I was thinking maybe we should go and meet her at the hospital."

"No, no. Reena is still in an unconscious state, which means she is in no condition to meet anyone, but this does not mean that Reena is in danger. As a matter of fact, she is completely out of danger. Treatment is going on, and after a few days, Reena will recover and will come out of the hospital. She is my responsibility now."

"Sir, I kept the gate and hotel door locked as you had said," Goverdhan Singh pitched in.

"Good."

"… and Sir, I apologize for talking to you like that yesterday; I shouldn't have talked like that,"

"No, Goverdhan ji, If I had been in your place, I would have probably done the same. There is no need to feel bad. And in fact, I should apologize to all of you for what happened yesterday. This was totally unexpected, some goons, antisocial, storming into the hotel like this… People whom I have never seen, let alone known, attacking my staff." Jaswant threw up his hands in exasperation.

"I shudder to think of what you, er, we have gone through. It is my fault that I have allowed this to happen and led you into this mess. I wouldn't have called you here if I had known that such things could happen …"

"How are you feeling today?" he asked, looking up at Bhopat.

"I am fine, Sir," Bhopat said, still looking dazed.

"There is nothing to fear right now. Those goons will get the harshest punishment. But with regret, I have to say that I took this decision." he paused for effect, keeping in mind your safety.

"Sir," Puspha interrupted. "After you left last night, we tried to check the CCTV footage, but all the cameras were switched off. We went to the storeroom to get the proof but."

"One minute. Are the CCTV cameras off? Jaswant asked incredulously.

"You are telling this now, for how many days?"

"Sir, the computer and DVR are in the storeroom. When I came to the storeroom the day before yesterday, the footage was showing, but surprisingly, it stopped last night."

"Let's go to the storeroom," Jaswant Kumar said, striding toward the storeroom.

Jaswant Kumar and Pushpa enter the storeroom. Pushpa switches on the computer, and multiple screens start showing no footage.

"Show me when it stopped yesterday."

Pushpa plays the footage in reverse, trying to go back to the time of the incident. "Show the footage here…" Jaswant Kumar points to a specific timeline.

"I want to know when exactly did it stop?"

Pushpa checked the footage timeline and said, "Sir, exactly tomorrow at 10:35 am."

"Cameras stop only when someone switches off the DVR. Right?"

"Yes, Sir, but there are cameras installed in the storeroom also, so if someone walked in to switch them off, we would have known in that case."

"Yesterday morning, someone came to the hotel; I mean, anyone from outside?" Jaswant asked.

"No. There was no one else except us," Pushpa said.

Jaswant Kumar fell silent for a while, lost in thought.

"Okay, thanks. Now do one thing: call all the staff members to the reception area." Pushpa hesitated.

"Is something else bothering you, Pushpa?"

"Sir, Jennifer seems very withdrawn."

"Where is she?"

"She has been sitting alone in her room since morning."

"Okay, tell her I have called. Everyone should be in the reception hall. I am coming in a while."

After around 5 minutes, Jaswant faces everyone in the reception area; the faces are long-drawn and fearful. A far cry from the enthusiastic, eager-to-please staff who had come to this hotel less than a month back.

"I am grateful and lucky to have a team like you. We worked hard and tried our best, but unfortunately, things did not go as per our expectations. And the incident that happened yesterday has shocked all of us, including me. I have decided to file a case against these goons who were part of this, and I will do my best to get them punished according to the law. But till then, your safety is my first priority, so keeping this in mind, I have decided to close the hotel for a few days. I'm really sorry about this affair; I've left you all disappointed. I wish I could continue this work," Jaswant said, spreading his hands. "Running the hotel. But for now, closing the hotel is the best option, keeping in mind your safety. As for Reena, I will stay with her until she recovers completely. I assure you that I will bear the full expenses of Reena's treatment. It may take a few days, but she will recover completely.

It is my responsibility to ensure Reena's recovery. And I am committed to it."

A mini-van draws up near the hotel gate.

"…I suggest you pack up your bags now; there is a van outside waiting to pick you up. The van will take you to the airport."

"Rinku?"

"Yes, Sir?"

"Since you are a local, the van will drop you to your house."

"Yes, Sir, I feel very bad leaving this place. You all became like my family, and I hate to leave…"

Jaswant Kumar interrupts him, "I can understand, but now you all start preparing. Here, this envelope contains all your tickets and some cash you may require for travel." He hands over an envelope to Pushpa.

The group gets up reluctantly; it is hard to tell if they are relieved to leave the impending danger or disappointed to leave their new job. They jostle to reach their rooms to pack their belongings and get away.

Jaswant is on the phone talking softly.

"It should be as I said."

"I know, I know, everyone has to get off at the airport; no staff should get off anywhere except the airport. Right?" Kaishav Jain repeats.

"Yes, explain it to the driver," Jaswant says.

"I have explained everything to the driver; my name is Kaishav Jain, and you know what? What I promise, I always deliver. There can't be any mistake in my work."

One by one, they climb onto the van, their bags already loaded; it's time to say final goodbyes.

When Jennifer walks toward the van, Jaswant Kumar calls out to her.

"Please, don't say anything to anyone. Please," he pleads.

Jennifer sits in the van without replying.

Jaswant Kumar shuts the gate, and the van starts moving toward Jaisalmer.

Jaswant Kumar goes to the hotel and closes the door from inside. He walks around silently, the wooden work on the furniture, the expensive paintings that adorn the walls, and the glorious chandelier. He walks through the maze of corridors, precariously putting forward each step on the carpeted floor, soaking in the luxury of the place, a place he has constructed brick by brick, curated each piece from the furniture, upholstery, paintings to the finest crockery… every damn thing he has picked up creating his dream hotel. He walked into one of the suite rooms, took in the plush decor, and for a few minutes stood in front of the AC darts to cool himself. He then went and looked at himself in the mirror, staring at his image.

After a while, he was back at the reception, staring at the large wall clock mounted above the reception desk. He stared at it, thinking.

He then pulled up a chair, stood against the walls, and turned the hands of the clock so that all hands pointed to 12.

After a while and some more reflection, he checked the call numbers listed on the reception phone and then picked up the phone while dialing a number.

"Hello, this is Mr Jaswant Kumar calling from The Titan Hotel… Is this Reena's residence?"

"And how are you related to Reena? … Okay, this is the owner of this hotel… I will definitely talk to Reena. We have sent Reena to Delhi for an important assignment for the hotel… yes, she has to be there for a few days, and she left behind her phone at the hotel by mistake… Yes, we can't tell how many days she will be back, but the rough estimate is around 15 days. … No, no, you don't need to worry; your daughter is absolutely safe and fine. She has gone to Delhi and will come soon… … Yes, as soon as she comes, I will ask her to call you. Yes. Thank you."

Jaswant Kumar locks the main door of the hotel and then the gate. Standing outside, he stares long and hard at the lightboard with The Titan Hotel Sign. Finally, he sits in the car and starts toward Jaisalmer.

Location: 7B, Shastri Nagar, Jaisalmer

Time: 5:15 (Evening)

The situation at his home needs to be assessed. He drives down to the place and, getting out of his car, quietly walks up to it. He realizes the front door is locked, so he walks around the tiny lawn and peeps through the window. Just then, Phoolan Devi calls from behind.

Phoolan Devi – "Kumarji?"

Jaswant Kumar pretends not to hear her, but Phoolan Devi is insistent; she slowly walks up to him even as Jaswant reaches his car.

"Kumarji, where were you? And where is Vaishali? You guys suddenly disappeared."

Jaswant Kumar: "Oh yes, some of our relatives are visiting, so we went to a common relative's place to spend time together.

Phoolan Devi: "Thank God. I got scared… last night some people came to your house. Once I thought that maybe they were known to you, I thought I would go and check on them. They looked odd. I was nervous. … but then I came to know that he is Kalu."

Jaswant Kumar: "Kalu?"

Phoolan Devi: "Yes, Kalu. He lived here before you. Then they disappeared suddenly. Saw him after many years. He recognized me as soon as he saw me. When asked about you, he did not answer anything. What is your relationship with Kalu?"

"But when we came here for the first time, the house was empty?" Jaswant said, surprised.

"That's what I am saying. The house was closed after he left. I don't remember that much, but…" Phoolan Devi left the words hanging in the air.

Jaswant Kumar: (seeing straightforward) "Nice to meet you, Phoolan Deviji. I have work to do now."

Location: Jain Real Estate, Jaisalmer

Time: 6:00 PM

Jaswant Kumar briskly arrives in a car and stands in front of Jain Real Estate. In a fit of anger, he opens the door and strides toward Kaishav Jain.

Kaishav Jain: "Oh, Jaswant Kumar! You shouldn't have come like this. A formal appointment was necessary…"

In anger, Jaswant Kumar approaches Kaishav Jain and grabs his collar, pushing him against the wall.

Jaswant Kumar: "You scoundrel, do you know how much trouble you've caused me?"

Kaishav Jain: (breathing heavily) "What have I done?"

Jaswant Kumar: "You've messed up my life."

Kaishav Jain: "Let go of my collar, I can't breathe. Look, we can talk peacefully…"

Jaswant Kumar: "You want to talk peacefully?"

Jaswant Kumar lifts the briefcase nearby and slams it on the table.

Kaishav Jain: (nervously) "No… don't do that, please. I had my reasons."

Jaswant Kumar: "You manipulated the land deal for that disputed property, and then you handed me Kalu Singh's house without any heads-up. That's quite the move; you really had your reasons, didn't you… But did you ever stop to consider what this would mean for my family?"

Kaishav Jain: "Let me explain. If I had refused, someone else would have taken that land. You knew it was valuable. I never forced you."

Jaswant Kumar: "And that guarantee about Kalu Singh's land? It was you to tell me that he won't return."

Kaishav Jain: "Let me tell you, even if I had refused, you would have taken that house. You knew it was prime property. I didn't force you. So, please calm down."

Jaswant Kumar puts the briefcase back on the table.

Jaswant Kumar: "How did you know that I would still buy the house?"

Kaishav Jain: "I recognize people at first glance. You may act, but deep down, you're a risk-taker. On the surface, a simple, ordinary guy; beneath, a daring player in life's high-stakes game. You don't take risks, but you yourself is a risk."

Jaswant Kumar: "Is that so?"

Kaishav Jain: "I didn't make these decisions without understanding. There were other houses in Jaisalmer, but they were not suitable. You are a family man. That's why I suggested this house."

Suddenly, the room fell silent. Both Kaishav Jain and Jaswant Kumar stopped talking, the tension between them palpable. Kaishav noticed a dramatic change in Jaswant's demeanor. The worried look on Jaswant's face disappeared, replaced by a calculated, confident expression. His eyes narrowed, focused, and his jaw set firmly. It was clear to Kaishav that Jaswant was no longer just reacting to the situation; he was thinking and planning. This is the second side of Jaswant Kumar that Kaishav had never seen before.

Jaswant Kumar: "Can you do one thing for me? Tell me the complete history of Kalu Singh. From start to end."

Chapter 7

Execution and Delivery

The sun had just begun to cast its morning glow upon the Government Registration Office in Jaisalmer, creating a sense of urgency in the air. The clock read 09:30 as Jaswant Kumar stormed into the office, completely disregarding any need for permission or courtesy. Bhakti Rajpurohit, attempting to halt his unannounced entrance, found herself in the midst of an unexpected confrontation.

"Oh, wait in line first…" Bhakti Rajpurohit insisted as Jaswant Kumar pressed forward.

"Madam, it's urgent…" Jaswant Kumar

"This is not my problem. Wait in line," Bhakti Rajpurohit sternly replied, determined to uphold the order.

Angrily, Jaswant Kumar retorted, "I don't have time; let me go in now."

"Hey! Do you understand? Move back…" Bhakti Rajpurohit stood her ground, facing the unyielding Jaswant Kumar.

In the ensuing struggle, Jaswant Kumar's forceful attempts to enter the office resulted in Bhakti Rajpurohit being pushed against the door, causing it to swing open. Chhagan Singh, witnessing the scene, promptly rushed to her aid.

(Anxiously) "I don't want to sell land and hotels… Cancel the form…" Jaswant Kumar urgently pleaded.

Concerned for Bhakti Rajpurohit, Chhagan Singh asked, "Are you okay??"

"Yes," Bhakti Rajpurohit responded, shaken but unharmed.

"Please don't process it. I don't want to sell anything, not a single thing…" Jaswant Kumar continued to express his distress.

Interrupting Jaswant Kumar, Chhagan Singh sternly stated, "Keep it quiet. This isn't your daddy's private playground where you stroll in whenever the mood strikes. You're treading on government turf now, and we play by the rules here. Pay attention, kid. You may have faced bigger and bigger goons in your life, but don't make this mistake with me. don't go thinking you can pull the stunt with me. I'm still playing nice, but that's for your own damn sake. Consider this your final warning. Show some damn respect, apologize to the lady."

Jaswant Kumar: (To Bhakti Rajpurohit) "Sorry."

Chhagan Singh: "Apologize for the misbehavior today; tell her it will never happen again."

Jaswant Kumar: (To Bhakti Rajpurohit) "What happened to you was wrong. And it will never happen again. It was my mistake, and I apologize for this."

Chhagan Singh: "Now, do you know what you'll do? With proper conduct, like a responsible citizen, you'll leave. Write your name on the desk, just like people waiting. You'll wait for your turn to come. Understand?"

Location: Tools Shop, Jaisalmer

Time: 10:30 AM

Jaswant Kumar signaled the shopkeeper outside the tools shop and honked his car horn. The door of the shop opened, and the shopkeeper came out with a bag. Jaswant got out of the car, opened the trunk and kept the bag in the trunk.

Shopkeeper: "Jain Sir must have briefed you. But listen, once you leave here, I don't know you, and you don't know me?" (Handing a card to Jaswant) "If caught, questioned, say you bought these 3 days ago."

Jaswant Kumar: "Who is this?"

Shopkeeper: "A hacker who used to order shady stuff online from dark websites abroad."

Jaswant Kumar: "Even mentioning his name could be trouble."

Shopkeeper: "If he's still breathing. 2 days ago, he met his end in an accident. Now, move your ass from here quickly, and don't show your face around here again."

Location: Joseph Property Construction Lines

Time: 10 AM

Don Robert surveyed the room, his sharp gaze fixed on Bindu. "What happened? Speak up again."

Bindu, feeling the weight of the moment, bowed his head. "Need to cancel the contract."

Don Robert let out a laugh that echoed through the material storage hall. "Cancel? Some people take business as a joke." He turned to his associates, "The cement has already left Mumbai."

Bindu, desperate to convey the urgency, pleaded, "Please stop it, Robertji. The other party has closed the hotel."

"That's his problem," Don Robert dismissed with a wave.

"He doesn't have the money," Bindu confessed.

Don Robert, unyielding, retorted, "Who is he? I know you. Not him. See, the whole world recognizes Don Robert by his work and words. I'm here today because I value my words more than money. I won't sell anything you wouldn't buy yourself. I gave you a 15-day deadline. Now you have 3 days. Bring 3.5 in 3 days."

As the scene shifted, Don Robert engaged in discussions with his associates, leaving Bindu standing tense with a bowed head. In the midst of their conversations, Robert observed Bindu wrestling with a dilemma.

Don Robert, breaking away from his associates, addressed them with urgency, "2 minutes."

Approaching Bindu, Don Robert placed a reassuring hand on his shoulder. "Look, Bindu, you're a good lad. Very straightforward. On your request, I've paid the guy up front. So, the deal won't be canceled. But yes, I can do one thing for you. I won't send cement and concrete; I'll stop the trucks. But you'll have to pay. 3 days. Alright?"

Bindu, overwhelmed and on the verge of tears, pleaded, "Please."

"My child," Don Robert softened, "fear is visible in your eyes. It's good because fear is the best way to avoid accidents. Don't let go of this fear."

Bindu emerged from Joseph Property Construction Lines, his steps quick and determined. Retrieving his phone, he dialed Jaswant Kumar.

Bindu: (on the phone) "Where are you?"

Jaswant Kumar: (driving) "Oh, thank God, I was about to call you…"

Bindu: (interrupting in anger) "I need money. Do you freaking understand? 3.5 crores, and that too today. I mean today."

Jaswant Kumar: "Okay, we need to meet urgently, in a deserted place. Tell me where to come."

Bindu: "Let me think…"

Jaswant Kumar: "We don't have much time."

Bindu: "Yes, Ram Setu Maidan. Just ahead of Ram Bagh Nursery… do you get it?"

Jaswant Kumar: (interrupting) "Yes, I know Ram Setu. I've been living in Jaisalmer for 2 years now."

Bindu: "Fine, I'll wait. Waiting for the money."

Jaswant Kumar hangs up the phone.

Under the relentless gaze of the desert sun, Jaswant Kumar, still behind the wheel, continued the conversation.

Jaswant Kumar: (on the phone) "Listen, I'm going out for a few days. Until then, stay in the hotel and…"

Vaishali Kumar: (interrupting) "What! Where are you going?"

Jaswant Kumar: "I have some work; it's necessary to go."

Vaishali Kumar: (interrupting) "Have you lost your mind? We're alone here, and you're going out."

Jaswant Kumar: (getting annoyed) "I'm not going for leisure. I'm going to resolve the incident. Understand? I'm going so that we can live our lives normally again. Every time, you complicate things. Every time, I have to make you understand."

Vaishali Kumar: "Tell me one thing. Do you think it's right to leave us alone like this?"

Jaswant Kumar: "Our future depends on it."

In the vast emptiness of Ram Setu, Jaisalmer, the clock relentlessly ticked toward noon, casting a shadow on the arid landscape as Bindu stood alone, anxiously awaiting Jaswant Kumar's arrival. Abruptly, the roar of a car engine shattered the stillness, announcing Jaswant Kumar's imminent arrival. At a rapid pace, the vehicle steered toward Bindu, abruptly coming to a halt as Jaswant Kumar swung the car door open and stepped out, urgency etched on his face.

Jaswant Kumar: (in haste) "Hurry, get in the car. We need to go far."

Bindu: "Where is the money?"

Jaswant Kumar: "What money?"

Bindu: "What money! The 3.5 crores I contracted for."

Jaswant Kumar: "We can discuss all this in the car. We don't have time, so quickly get in."

Bindu: "So, you didn't bring the money?"

Jaswant Kumar: "Yes, is there a packet of biscuits I could have bought from the market?"

Bindu: "Oh, damn it! (yells) Give me the money now, from anywhere, I don't care. I went to that builder for you and took the risk in my name. He's not canceling the damn contract. I'll have to pay him under any circumstances."

Jaswant Kumar: "I don't have the money right now."

Bindu: "Then arrange from anywhere, you dumb shit. I don't know. I need the money, or else…"

Jaswant Kumar: (interrupting) "What's the problem with this? We can talk about all this in the car. Get in quickly."

Bindu: "You don't have any idea; he's Don Robert. If he doesn't get the money in 3 days, he'll kill me. I am the only support for my father. If something happens to me…"

Jaswant Kumar: (interrupting) "Calm down. Nothing like that will happen."

Bindu: "I plead, give me the money. That's it."

Jaswant Kumar: "Look, we're both trapped and in such a way that if we don't do anything now, everything will be ruined. Crying won't solve anything. Now, listen, I have a plan. If we succeed, I assure you nothing will happen to you. Trust me."

Bindu: "Trust? And that too in you. A man who burned his own staff member alive."

Jaswant Kumar: (angry) "She was dying. No matter how hard we tried, death was written in her fate. And neither you nor I could have saved her. If she hadn't been burned, we would be somewhere else today. I saved both of you. And now, about the current situation, our future is hanging by a thread that can snap at any moment. We have 2 options: either accept defeat and wait for death or find a solution to this problem and fight. And what we are about to do is the only and last way that can save us. Will you listen to my plan now?"

After a while

Bindu: "No, I'm not going to do this."

Jaswant Kumar: "We have to do this; we have no other option."

Bindu: "There's a risk in this. Doing all this is not easy. There's a difference between saying and doing. (getting frustrated) And again and again, why are you using the word 'we'? All this happened because of you. Because of you, I have to endure all this."

Jaswant Kumar: "Bindu, listen to me carefully. Maybe, in your perspective, I'm a bad person, but I'm the only one who can save you. This time, trust me, finally, trust me."

Bindu: "I never thought such days would come."

Jaswant Kumar: (angry) "The days are yet to come. This is just the beginning. So, let's do one thing: count the days. Wait for the arrival of Robert. I'm going. Because I want to live."

Bindu is thinking. Jaswant Kumar gets into the car. Bindu approaches.

Bindu: "Understand, this plan worked. So, what's in it for me?"

Jaswant Kumar: "Your benefit is my guarantee. I promise I won't let anything happen to you, even until my last breath. No matter what happens. Now, we either do this or we face destruction."

Under the relentless gaze of the scorching sun, Jaswant Kumar expertly steered the car through the dusty roads of Nachna, Bindu seated quietly by his side. The atmosphere inside the vehicle was thick with unspoken tension, occasionally disrupted by Bindu's discreet conversation over the phone.

Bindu: (on the phone) "I've prepared lunch; I need to serve lunch and dinner... Thanks, buddy; it might take me a couple of days... Please stay with him, and ensure he takes his medicines on time... You're a lifesaver, my friend… Alright, if anything comes up, I'll call you… Okay… Thanks… Bye."

Jaswant Kumar: "Who was that?"

Bindu: "My close friend, he lives nearby. Since Dad is alone at home, I need someone nearby to take care of him, provide food, and keep an eye on him."

Jaswant Kumar: "Anything urgent to call now?"

Bindu: "Why?"

Jaswant Kumar: "Because from now on, we're turning off our phones."

Bindu: "Turning off our phones?"

Jaswant Kumar: "We shouldn't do anything that could track us. Tomorrow, our phones might get traced. One piece of evidence is enough for them to put us in the suspect's circle."

The car came to a halt at a secluded spot by the road.

Jaswant Kumar: "Take out the SIM card from your phone and keep them in your pocket. Once the job is done, we'll come back to this spot."

Both Jaswant Kumar and Bindu extracted the SIM cards from their phones, securing them in their pockets.

Jaswant Kumar: "Bring your phone outside."

Bindu: "Now phone?"

They stood by the road near a tree, Jaswant Kumar digging into the ground with his hands.

Bindu: "What are you doing?"

Jaswant Kumar: (digging) "Phones can be tracked by IMEI, too, so I'm digging a hole. This way, both our phones will remain hidden here."

Bindu: "But how will you remember the exact spot when we come back?"

Jaswant Kumar: "Bindu, I may be 55, but my memory never fails. Turn off the phones before placing them in the hole. No one should see us hiding them."

Hours later, on Suratgarh Bikaner Road, Rajasthan, Bindu's stomach's growls broke the silence.

Bindu: "I'm hungry."

Jaswant Kumar: "There are some snacks in the back."

Bindu: "Snacks? Biscuits and chips? You didn't bring along a 10-year-old. Let's stop at a dhaba."

Jaswant Kumar: "No, we're not stopping anywhere. These are the rules."

Bindu: "This is amazing. You forced me to come, and now you're dictating the rules."

Jaswant Kumar: "Every decision has a reason. I don't want to cause you any trouble. I've been hungry since morning. We just need to be cautious. I don't want to put you in trouble or get stuck myself."

Bindu opened a packet of chips from the backseat.

Bindu: "And for how long?"

Jaswant Kumar: "Around 10 PM."

Bindu: "Yeah, then we'll find a good hotel, right? Then we can sleep comfortably. After all, we've traveled this far."

Jaswant Kumar: "Are we going for a picnic?"

Bindu: "You don't even want to take a hotel? Where will we sleep then? This is getting too much. I've been following your instructions for so long; it doesn't mean you can do whatever you want."

Jaswant Kumar: "Bindu, our slightest mistake can cost us. We need to be careful with every step. Understand that after an incident, the police will investigate, even in hotels, which is inevitable. Now, it's not challenging because Hanumangarh is a small town with selected hotels. The police will scrutinize, and Jaswant and Bindu from Jaisalmer will be under suspicion. You're talking about hotels; we need to avoid entering the city. A plan is successful when there's a 0% error. That's when it achieves perfect execution and delivery."

Bindu: "Execution and delivery?"

Jaswant Kumar: "Do you know what the most powerful thing in the world is? An idea. An idea that discovers light without rubbing stones, an idea that explores gravity without knowing nature's forces, an idea that can take humans to the moon. It's as powerful as it is dangerous. It's a virus that keeps spreading; it can either make you successful or completely destroy you. And for me, an idea that is not dangerous is not worthy of being called an idea. Plans are made from these ideas. Now, it's time for execution and delivery. Demonstrating and providing it, that's what I call execution and delivery."

Bindu: "You seem wise on one side and, on the other, heartless," he remarked.

Jaswant raised an eyebrow in question. "What do you mean?"

"That night, before spraying petrol, where were your thoughts, your big talks, your discipline, your humanity? Where were they?" Bindu asked, his voice laced with bitterness.

Jaswant's face remained impassive as he replied coolly, "The only difference is that you were thinking about the present, and I was thinking about the future."

Location: Suratgarh - Hanumangarh Road, Rajasthan

Time: 11:00 PM

Jaswant Kumar and Bindu cover their faces with handkerchiefs.

Jaswant Kumar: "Hanumangarh is 10 km from here. Pay attention; a road will come up ahead. We need to go from there."

After a while, Jaswant Kumar redirects the car onto a rough road that leads toward a small hill. After some time, they reach the top of the hill.

Bindu: "Now?"

Jaswant Kumar: "What do you mean?"

Bindu: "I mean, what's next?"

Jaswant Kumar said, "What now? Sleep in peace."

Bindu questioned, "In the car?"

Jaswant Kumar replied, "Imagine as if you're lying on a luxurious bed in a five-star hotel."

Bindu responded, "Wow, thank you. You've solved my problem. Keep this lousy imagination to yourself; it's better that way."

Jaswant Kumar advised, "Go to sleep; we have work from tomorrow. Right now, you need more rest."

With a sigh, Bindu settled back in his seat and closed his eyes, knowing that there was still a long road ahead for them both.

Location: Mehran Tekadi, Hanumangarh

Time: 7:00 AM (Next morning)

The sun rises over Mehran Tekadi, casting a warm glow as Bindu wakes up. Jaswant Kumar is busy removing equipment from the car's trunk.

"Good morning," Jaswant Kumar greets him with a serious smile.

Curiosity gets the better of Bindu. "What's all this for?"

Bindu's eyes widened as he examined the bag. "Binoculars and… a gun? Who's that for?"

Jaswant Kumar reassures him, "Don't worry, it's just a fake. In case of emergencies."

Bindu continues questioning, his voice shaky. "And what about this headset? Is it some kind of spy gadget?"

Jaswant Kumar: "It's a wireless walkie-talkie. Just put it in your ear, and no one will know."

As more items are revealed, including folding chairs, Bindu can't hide his sarcasm. "Are we planning on staying here for weeks? Because let me tell you, I have zero interest in staying here for more than 2 minutes."

Jaswant Kumar: "Come with me now."

Both stand at the mountain edge, looking down at a factory below.

Jaswant Kumar points out, "Can you see that?"

Bindu: "I am not blind. Of course, I can see it. It's the factory."

Jaswant Kumar replies, "We have to keep an eye on it. That's our mission."

Bindu questions further, "And then what? What comes next?"

Jaswant Kumar gestures for him to look through the binoculars and hands him another pair. "Just keep watching. It's crucial that we monitor their movements."

Bindu sighs, "You mean we're going to spend the whole day here just watching this factory? Is this why we came all this way?"

Jaswant Kumar insists, "It's necessary, Bindu. Our entire operation depends on this surveillance. Now, put on the binoculars and keep your eyes focused."

Both use the binoculars to observe the factory from a distance.

As they continue watching, Bindu is amazed at the clarity. "Wow, these are incredible! We can see everything so clearly from such a distance."

Jaswant Kumar explains, "Yes, it's a night vision telescope. It allows us to see even in the dark."

Hour's pass, but Bindu's patience wears thin.

"Enough is enough," he declares, his stomach grumbling. "I need some rest. And what about dinner? Oh, right, I forgot… chips and biscuits. I don't think I've eaten this much junk food since my childhood."

But Jaswant Kumar doesn't budge, his eyes still glued to the binoculars. "You can go whenever you want, but please don't distract me."

Bindu scoffs in frustration. "Why not? The Taj Mahal is standing right in front of you, keep starring."

Sitting on a folding chair, eating chips, and Jaswant Kumar joins on another chair a while later.

Bindu asked, "What happened? Didn't you like the Taj Mahal?"

Jaswant Kumar replied, "Intermission break."

Bindu: "You look quite tired."

Jaswant Kumar hesitated, "Well… just like that."

Bindu: "Here, have some chips."

Jaswant Kumar declined, "No, these are for you."

Bindu insisted, "You haven't eaten anything since yesterday. Take these biscuits, then."

Jaswant Kumar refused, "No. The stock is low. If I eat, there won't be any left for you."

Bindu: "No problem. You need it more than I do."

Jaswant Kumar: "Bindu… please, no. I don't want to eat."

Bindu agreed, "Alright then."

Jaswant Kumar starts to leave.

Bindu suggested, "Take a short break."

Jaswant Kumar: "NO."

After a while, Bindu, holding binoculars, joins Jaswant Kumar.

Location: Mehran Tekadi, Hanumangarh

Time: 1:00 (Night)

Jaswant Kumar and Bindu are sitting in the car.

Jaswant Kumar explained, "This is the leather factory where shoes, jackets, etc., are made. The guard opens the factory gate sharp at 8 am. Work starts at 9 am. Around 10 am, the goods are loaded onto trucks."

Bindu interrupted, "And about 12 trucks were parked there."

Jaswant Kumar continued, "Yes, 12 trucks are loaded with goods. After loading, each truck goes in a different direction toward the villages around the city. After supplying goods to the villages, the empty trucks return to the factory. The trucks start coming around 8 PM, and the last truck arrives at 11 PM. Because it goes to Bikaner, which is far from here. So, there's no chance it will come back quickly. It comes from the Peelipanga route. And at night, that road is deserted. No one coming, no one going. Only that one truck and no one else."

Bindu acknowledged, "Yes."

Jaswant Kumar continued, "And there's a tea shop right next to the factory. The factory employees go there to have tea. That shop closes at 9 PM. Before 9 PM, that will be your time."

Bindu replied, "Got it."

Time: 8:30 (Next Night)

The car is parked in a deserted field, the only sounds coming from the distant howling of coyotes. Bindu covers his face with a handkerchief, pulling it tight over his nose and mouth, obscuring his features. He then adds another jacket on top of his already layered clothing.

Jaswant Kumar: "Put on another one."

Bindu: "I'm already wearing 2 jackets."

Jaswant Kumar: "Trust me, you don't want to risk being identified. Cover your face completely. And did you grab the wallet?"

Bindu: "Yes."

Jaswant Kumar: "Good. Remember what we talked about."

Bindu: "Yes."

Jaswant Kumar: "Alright, get to work."

Location: Paramount Works Factory, Hanumangarh.

Time: 8:45 (Night)

Bindu cautiously approaches the nearby tea stall, scanning the area for any signs of security or witnesses.

Bindu: "How much is the tea?"

Shopkeeper: "10 rupees."

Bindu reaches into his pockets and pulls out a 100–rupee note.

Bindu: "Give me a cup."

The shopkeeper hesitates, eyeing Bindu's makeshift disguise warily.

Shopkeeper: "Do you have change?"

Bindu shakes his head and takes the cup of tea anyway.

Bindu: "Can I sit inside?"

Shopkeeper: "Yes, but quickly… I'll give you change."

Bindu accepts the shopkeeper's words and sits at a table. Threw the entire tea out the window. He deliberately and carefully drops a wallet from his pocket on the floor. A calculated move follows as Bindu stands up and rushes out of the tea stall.

Shopkeeper (calling after him): "Hey brother, your change!

Location: 6 kilometers before Hanumangarh

Time: 9:15 (Night)

Jaswant Kumar: "What happened?"

Bindu: "The job is done."

Jaswant Kumar: "Okay! Now, the next stage. Hurry, get in the car."

Location: Suratgarh Hanumangarh Road, Rajasthan

Time: 11:30 (Night)

A truck speeds down a deserted road, the only source of light coming from its headlights. The driver taps his fingers on the steering wheel as he listens to music blaring on the radio. Suddenly, his eyes widen in shock as he spots a fallen tree blocking the road ahead.

Bindu, hidden in the bushes with binoculars, watches and relays information through a walkie-talkie.

Bindu (urgently): "He's gotten out of the truck… wait for my signal… now! Move quickly!"

Jaswant Kumar sprints toward the truck from the roadside. Meanwhile, the truck driver struggles to move the heavy tree blocking his path. Jaswant Kumar skilfully retrieves a bomb and cable ties from the bag hidden under the truck. Across the road, the driver finally manages to clear the tree.

Bindu (frantically): "He's cleared it; hurry up!"

Jaswant Kumar (struggling to tie the bomb): "I can't get it to stay on properly; it keeps slipping!"

Bindu (desperately): "Just do something, he's coming back!"

With trembling hands, Jaswant Kumar finally secures the bomb onto the fuel tank and starts to make his escape.

Bindu (breathless): "No, no, don't come out yet, he's turning back."

In a rush of fear, Jaswant Kumar quickly hides under the truck. At that moment, the driver climbs into the truck and turns on the engine. Suddenly, the phone in the driver's pocket starts ringing.

Truck Driver (on phone): "Hello? What's going on? A tree has blocked my route… I'll be there soon… okay."

While the driver is on the phone, Jaswant Kumar scrambles out from underneath the truck and runs for cover in the darkness.

Location: Mehran Tekadi, Hanumangarh

Time: 12:00 (Night)

Both figures crouch low on the rooftop, their eyes trained on the factory in front of them as they peer through binoculars. Bindu's voice is tense with anticipation.

Bindu: "Where is our truck parked?"

Jaswant Kumar: "Over there. See the second one from the left."

Bindu: "Is this really going to work?"

Jaswant Kumar: "With 260 kilograms of RDX, it has to. This leather factory will put up a fierce resistance, but we need to ensure maximum damage."

Bindu: "So you knew all along that this was a leather factory."

Jaswant Kumar: "Of course. I always do my research."

The sound of metal clinking against metal fills the air as Jaswant Kumar retrieves a small device from his bag.

Bindu: "What is that?"

Jaswant Kumar: "A remote. With just one press of a button…"

But he is cut off by Bindu's eager interruption.

Bindu: "Wow, tell me more about how it works."

Jaswant Kumar's voice turns serious as he warns Bindu not to play around with the device.

Jaswant Kumar: "This isn't a toy. Just look, but don't touch the button."

Bindu pouts but nods obediently.

Bindu: "I've seen things like this in movies. So, when are we going to… you know… press the button?"

Jaswant Kumar shakes his head.

Jaswant Kumar: "Not yet. We have to wait until everyone has left the factory. We don't want to hurt anybody."

After some time.

Jaswant Kumar peeks through the binoculars again.

Jaswant Kumar: "The coast is clear. Everyone has left, and the guard has locked up."

Bindu: "Can we do it now?"

Jaswant Kumar: "Yes. Get ready."

Bindu's voice quivers with fear and doubt.

Bindu: "What if something goes wrong? What if we get caught?"

But Jaswant Kumar doesn't have time to reassure him as he presses the button on the device, Bindu covering his own ears with his hands.

Bindu: "What happened? Why isn't it working?"

Jaswant Kumar continues to press the button frantically, panic creeping into his voice.

Jaswant Kumar: "I don't understand! It should work!"

Bindu suggests checking the batteries, but Jaswant Kumar's anger flares.

Jaswant Kumar: "This doesn't use batteries, you fool!"

Finally, in a fit of frustration, Jaswant Kumar slumps down on the rooftop, holding his head in his hands.

Jaswant Kumar: "Everything is ruined. We are finished, Bindu. (Holding up the device) We put all our faith in this, and yet it failed us. And this… this useless button…"

Suddenly, a deafening explosion rocks the air, accompanied by intense heat and blinding light. The factory erupts into flames, the ground shaking beneath them.

Jaswant Kumar and Bindu watch in awe and horror as their plan unfolds before their eyes.

Jaswant Kumar: "I never thought it would be this intense."

But soon, the sound of sirens pierces through the chaos.

Jaswant Kumar: "We have to leave. Now. Before someone catches us."

In a frenzy, they gather their things and run from the rooftop as they hear voices approaching.

The scene fades to black as they disappear into the night, leaving behind a trail of destruction and chaos.

Chapter 8

The Snake

Jaswant Kumar stands outside room 89, ringing the doorbell frantically. Vaishali Kumar opens the door with a worried expression.

Jaswant Kumar (breathless): "Thank God you're okay."

Vaishali Kumar gets away without responding, leaving Jaswant standing in the doorway. Inside, Mihir Kumar is engrossed in a mobile game. Jaswant's face falls as he sees his son's disinterested demeanor.

Jaswant Kumar (trying to remain calm): "How are you, son?"

Mihir Kumar remains silent, his fingers moving quickly on the screen. Jaswant persists, "What game is this? Mihir? Are you upset?"

Mihir Kumar (finally looking up): "Where were you, Papa?"

Jaswant Kumar's heart sinks at the hurt in his son's voice. He takes a seat beside Mihir, trying to compose himself.

Jaswant Kumar: "Me? I was at my hotel; I had some work. A lot of it. It's finally done now."

Mihir Kumar (voice breaking): "You weren't at the hotel."

Jaswant Kumar's eyes widen in shock and guilt.

Jaswant Kumar: "What do you mean?"

Mihir Kumar: "Do you lie, Papa? Mom told me everything. You left us like this. Why did you do that?"

Cut to Vaishali Kumar, seated in the living room, reading a book with tear tracks on her cheeks. Jaswant, angry and desperate for answers, confronts her.

Jaswant Kumar (angry): "What did you tell Mihir?"

Vaishali Kumar continues reading, seemingly ignoring him.

Jaswant Kumar (frustrated): "Vaishali? I am asking you something. What did you tell Mihir?"

Vaishali remains silent for a moment before slowly looking up at Jaswant, her eyes brimming with emotion.

Vaishali Kumar: "That you went on a trip."

Jaswant Kumar (voice rising): "Just that? What was the need for all those?"

Vaishali Kumar: "Don't shout. You disappeared without a trace for 3 whole days. Your phone was switched off. Can you even begin to imagine the fear and worry we went through? And now, your son. Questions after questions. Where is Papa? What answer do I give him?"

Jaswant Kumar, his voice laced with anger, snapped, "Why did you have to spill? You could've simply said he's away for important business or working at the hotel."

Vaishali, resolute and unyielding, retorted, "You can lie to your son; I couldn't. You were missing for 3 days," Vaishali says, her voice laced with anger and hurt. "My calls went unanswered; your phone was switched off. I was alone, wondering where you were, if you were okay."

Jaswant Kumar: "Where do you think I was? Jodhpur. The police transferred the case there. Why? I don't know. Suddenly, I received a call saying I had to go to the Jodhpur police station. Now, I had 2 options: either ignore it and face penalties in the future, or immediately go to the station and settle the case. I know how I faced every question of the police for 3 days. Only I know in what condition I emerged from this trouble. This fight started with a trivial matter, but those goons had a political background, which escalated the situation, forcing me to go to Jodhpur. I fought with them alone for 3 days. Why? So that under any circumstances, everything returns to normal. So that my family remains safe. And you? sightseeing? Who dumb human can go for a picnic in this situation? It's been so many years since our marriage, yet you still can't recognize me."

Vaishali Kumar: "Alright. I understand, Jaswant. I understand everything, but if you had just informed me over the phone, I wouldn't have had to go through this ordeal. You sat there with your phone switched off. Do you know what thoughts were running through my mind?"

Jaswant Kumar: "The phone was discharged, and there were no facilities to charge it. Vaishali, every step, every decision, every plan of mine is aimed at somehow protecting my family. So that I can run a successful hotel. Do you know why? Because our entire future is invested in that hotel. And you, who constantly doubts me. Always questioning my decisions, making a mockery of my self-confidence."

Vaishali Kumar: "Because I've paid the price. I've emerged from such situations and seen so much pain. Those days haunt me, and I don't want to relive them. That's why I'm always worried. I don't care about myself; I care about our child."

Jaswant Kumar: (interrupting) "I, too, care for him, but you still won't believe me. Explaining to you is like banging one's head on the wall."

Vaishali Kumar: "Ever since the hotel opened, I have seen you investing money. You say rooms are full, but I don't see that."

Jaswant Kumar: "Hardly 2 months have passed since the hotel opened. Yes, the rooms are full, but the expenses are as much as the income. If you want everything in 2 months, then let me tell you, it is impossible. Have some patience. I need some time, and then the grand Titan Hotel would be standing in the blooming air in the middle of the desert."

Vaishali Kumar: "You return after 3 days; everything must be resolved by now. I want to go home. I can't stay in this room any longer."

Jaswant Kumar: "No, not now. There are still a few things left. But we'll leave soon, just a matter of a few days. Let things settle first."

Vaishali Kumar: "I'll see about that. For now, the bathroom is open; take a shower. What condition have you come back in… Were you at the police station or stranded somewhere in the desert? Go… and I hope your decision is the right one."

Jaswant Kumar: "If you still hope, then you don't know me."

Location: 512, Gandhi Nagar, Jaisalmer

Time: 11:30 AM

(On the phone)

Bindu: "Good morning, Sir. Bindu speaking."

Kaishav Jain: "Oh, Bindu, hi! How are you?"

Bindu: "Sir, I need some help. I need some money. You're the only one I can rely on. Please, Sir, I hope you won't say no."

Kaishav Jain: "Hope! My job is all about that, I hope. And hope is what leads to money. And who in this world doesn't need money? Take my example: I need money, too. And when I need money, how can I help you?"

Bindu: (Angry) "I've been your vendor for 3 years. Despite having so much work, you never gave me a chance. I've been sitting here all these years, relying only on you. And today, I'm asking for help…"

Kaishav Jain: (Interrupting) "Who said I haven't given you clients? All were like ants, Bindu. I gave you the elephant… Jaswant Kumar, a 50-crore project."

Bindu: (Interrupting, angrily) "And you took a 9% commission. What could have been done in 42? You stretched to 46. And what did I get? 4 lakhs? You gave me just 4 lakhs out of 46 crores."

Kaishav Jain: (Interrupting) "Work calmly. You are new, but with time, you will get more clients and income. Remember, you are associated with Jain Real Estate and our…"

Bindu: (Interrupting angrily) "Forget your real estate and forget you. Let me tell you something: from tomorrow, turn this into Jain Fake Estate. Because it suits you better…"

Suddenly, a noise is heard from behind. Bindu rushes to the next room, where Pokhar has fallen unconscious from the bed. Bindu picks him up in a state of unconsciousness and lays him on the bed.

"Father?" Bindu's voice quivered, fear gripping his heart. "Father, please wake up!" But the silence that followed was deafening. Frantic, he grabbed his phone, his fingers trembling as he dialed the emergency number. "Please, I need an ambulance at 512, Gandhi Nagar. Hurry!" he pleaded, his voice.

Location: Shankar Cloth Laundry, Jaisalmer

Time: 12 PM

Amidst the whir of machines and the busy hum of workers, the factory owner sat sternly at his desk. His gaze was unwavering, his demeanor unyielding.

Just then, Jaswant Kumar entered, his presence a stark contrast to the order of the factory. "I need to see Aslam," he said.

The Factory Owner: "Leave now. Visitors are not permitted during working hours."

As Jaswant hesitated, Aslam emerged from the shadows, a friendly smile on his face. "This is my friend," he explained to the factory owner, attempting to ease the tension.

The factory owner pointed to a sign that read, 'No visitors during working hours.' Aslam: "Why don't we go outside (to the owner)? Give me just 2 minutes.

After both coming out, Jaswant's voice was heavy with regret. "I didn't know the land belonged to Kalu Singh," he confessed. "It was all a misunderstanding. I just want to apologize."

Aslam: "Kalu Singh isn't here. He's in jail; he was bailed for a day. Now tell me, who told you about this place?"

Jaswant Kumar: "I am leaving Jaisalmer forever, today itself. I just want an assurance."

Aslam: "What kind of assurance?"

Jaswant Kumar: "Assurance that my family will be safe."

Aslam: "I've never seen such a dumb person like u before. First, you grabbed his land, and beyond that, you conquered his house too. A fool? No, a clown in the court of danger, that's what you are," he sneered. "Staying in Jaisalmer after your blunder? That's not just foolish, it's suicidal. Death is looming over you, and look at you, you are still here."

Jaswant Kumar: "I am an ordinary person, I didn't know…

He leaned in closer, his voice dropping to a growl. "Here's my only advice: vanish. Disappear from this city like a shadow at dawn; if you care for your family and if you dare to step foot here again in this area, remember this: my leniency has an expiration date, and trust me, you don't want to be around when the clock runs out."

After giving this warning, Aslam goes toward the factory. Jaswant stands there thinking something, and a smile appears on his face like it's part of a plan.

Location: R.L. Memorial Hospital, Jaisalmer

Time: 12:30 PM

The atmosphere was tense and full of worry as Bindu's father was quickly taken into the ICU. Bindu stood outside, looking very worried. After a while, a nurse guided him to the receptionist's desk.

The receptionist looked up as Bindu approached. "Is Bindu your name?" she asked in a routine tone.

"Yes," Bindu replied, his voice laced with anxiety.

"And how is the patient related to you?"

"He's, my father."

The receptionist handed him a form. "Alright. Please fill this out."

"Will my father be, okay?"

"I cannot say for sure. The doctors will inform you," the receptionist replied, maintaining her professional demeanor. "Please fill out this form and make a payment of 70 thousand."

The amount struck Bindu like a thunderbolt. "How much?"

"70 thousand, Sir."

Bindu was lost in thought for a moment, then said, "I'll be back in 2 minutes."

The receptionist's response was firm but empathetic. "What happened? Sir, don't take too long. Proper treatment begins only after the fee is paid."

Location: Jain Real Estates

Time: 1:00 PM

Bindu went to Jain Real Estates, hoping to find help for his urgent problem. The owner, Kaishav Jain, was surprised to see him come in so suddenly.

"Hey, Bindu! You can't come inside without permission?"

Bindu, nerves frayed and voice shaky, blurted out, "I need some money urgently, otherwise…"

Kaishav Jain, attempting to remind Bindu of their prior conversation, was interrupted. "Bindu, I've already informed you about this on the phone. Our policy…"

But Bindu, tears streaming down his face, cut him off. "My father is admitted to the hospital. It's an emergency. I don't have money for his treatment. If something happens to him… There will be nothing left behind me. Please help me. I'm begging…"

Kaishav Jain, hesitating at first, finally relented. "Okay, okay, how much do you need?"

"70 thousand," Bindu managed to say through his sobs.

Kaishav Jain quickly went to the safe and pulled out a stack of money. "Here, it's a total of 1 lakh."

"But I only need 70 thousand."

"Keep the extra, in case you need more. But remember, there will be 12% interest. Keep that in mind."

Bindu, overwhelmed by gratitude, managed to say, "Thank you very much"

Kaishav Jain urged him to hurry. "Don't delay now. Hurry."

As Bindu left, Kaishav Jain's voice followed him. "Take care of your father. And yes, there's no rush for the money. Pay it back when you're completely stable."

Location: The Titan Hotel

Time: 2:00 PM

Jaswant Kumar entered The Titan Hotel, his clothes dusted from the desert. In the reception hall, he paused, noticing a small, ominous bloodstain on the floor. A CCTV camera hung overhead, silently observing.

Acting swiftly, Jaswant grabbed a chair and stood on it to open the camera, which had wiring connected to each other. Studied the tangled wires, then moved to the storage room. There, he found more wires leading from the DVR through the walls.

Jaswant was determined to find a spot not covered by the cameras. He started tapping the walls, listening for empty spaces. When he suspected wires were hidden behind the plaster, he used a hammer to break through. He made hole after hole in the wall, but each time, he only found more wires. After hours of this exhausting search, Jaswant felt defeated. He sat down, tired and sweating, feeling like he had failed. After a while, he felt like peeing; as he went to the bathroom, something caught his eye. On a shelf, there was a black cap box. Jaswant used a chair to reach it, opened it with his screwdriver, and found cut wires inside – exactly what he was looking for.

Excited, Jaswant rushed back to the storage room and turned on the computer. He loaded the footage from the camera outside the bathroom. The screen showed Rinku entering the bathroom. Then, just a few minutes later, the footage suddenly stopped. The camera had been turned off at a crucial moment. Jaswant realized he had found a key piece of evidence in his investigation.

Jaswant Kumar: (On the phone) "I need to meet you right away."

Kaishav Jain: "I have clients in front of me, not today."

Jaswant Kumar: (Angrily) "It's urgent. Meet me in Joga in 2 hours, in front of the Hanuman Temple. Understand? Open your ears and be there."

Location: Joga, Jaisalmer

Time: 6:00 PM

Jaswant Kumar had driven to the agreed meeting spot, his car stirring up clouds of dust in its wake. Kaishav Jain followed closely, his car's engine growling in the quiet desert evening. They both came to a stop in a desolate area, far from prying eyes.

Kaishav Jain emerged from his car, visibly irritated. "I am not your puppet, Jaswant," he spat out. "I had to leave clients mid-negotiation for this. You know, a deal worth 68 lakhs. If they walk because of your urgency, you're covering 35% of my loss."

Jaswant Kumar didn't let him finish. "Oh, you're worried about your losses?" he interrupted, sarcasm lacing his tone. "Think about those who suffer from your deceit."

Kaishav Jain bristled. "I deserve respect, Mr. Kumar. I'm not here to be insulted. Let's talk like civilized people, or…"

But Jaswant cut him off again, his voice rising in anger. "Civil talk? With you? A man who'd cross any line for money? How much did you take from Kalu Singh?"

Confusion and anger flashed across Kaishav Jain's face. "Money from Kalu Singh? What kind of nonsense are you talking about?"

Jaswant leaned in; his voice intense. "Rinku. The boy you sent to work at the hotel. He was Kalu Singh's man. 2 months he spent there, pretending to be an innocent worker."

Kaishav Jain's: "Rinku? I don't know any Rinku."

Jaswant shook his head in frustration. "Of course, you don't know him just like you don't remember the other staff you sent. Convenient memory, huh?"

Kaishav Jain stood his ground, his voice firm and steady as he addressed Jaswant Kumar. "Mr Kumar, listen carefully and don't interrupt," he began a note of authority in his tone. "I run Jain Real Estates, and my business hinges on a network of vendors. The vendor's job is simple: they fulfill the customer's needs. For instance, if you wanted a new car tomorrow, I'd contact my vendor. They'd source the car and deliver it straight to you, like home delivery, hassle-free. In the same way, when I needed 6 professional hotel staff, I relayed this to my vendor. They, in turn, used their contacts to fulfill my request. Do you think I personally go around recruiting? I have numerous clients, countless vendors, and a variety of services to manage. It's impossible for me to remember every name."

Kaishav's expression grew more intense. "And think about it: if I were really Kalu Singh's man, why would I have disclosed his entire background to you? That doesn't make sense. I'm just a businessman, not some puppet in a grand conspiracy."

Jaswant Kumar: "Did you tell your vendor these staff were for The Titan Hotel?"

Kaishav Jain shook his head. "I just give them my requirements. I don't share client details. It's a rule. And no, I know nothing about your staff or this Rinku."

Jaswant in frustration. "He sabotaged the hotel, turned off cameras, and helped Kalu Singh. It was all a setup."

Kaishav Jain: "It seems you are part of some conspiracy, too, Mr. Kumar. You're no different in this game. Thanks for ruining my evening and wasting my time." With that, he turned and walked back to his car, leaving Jaswant Kumar alone with his thoughts and the growing darkness.

Location: Empire Hotel, Jaisalmer

Time: 9:30 PM

Jaswant Kumar stood outside the Empire Hotel; his phone held to his ear. In the dim light of the streetlamp. "I'm sorry for being so rude earlier"

Kaishav Jain's voice came through, calm and understanding. "No need to apologize. We're businessmen; disagreements are part of our work. They help us find the right solutions. And if I say true, I'm used to it."

Jaswant hesitated, then asked, "Can I ask you something?"

"Sure," replied Kaishav.

"Will our plan actually work?"

Kaishav Jain: "I can't really say. The plan was your idea. I just gave you the information you wanted."

Jaswant nodded to himself, unseen by Kaishav. "Goodnight," he said quietly.

"Goodnight, Mr. Kumar," Kaishav responded before the line went dead.

Location: Jain Real Estate, Jaisalmer

Time: 9:35 PM

Kaishav Jain stood by his office window, looking out at the evening sky. The sky had turned an eerie red, and the wind was picking up. "Strange," he murmured to himself, "I've never seen weather like this in the city before. It feels like a storm is about to hit."

Location: Suratgarh – Bikaner Road, Rajasthan

Time: 8:00 AM (Next Morning)

The next morning, a snake slithered alongside a deserted road near Suratgarh. It was searching for food, moving quickly toward a nearby field. Just then, a bus thundered past, disturbing the quiet of the morning.

The bus was packed with passengers. Every seat was taken, and many people were standing in the aisles. Among them stood a man with a noticeable presence. He had a charming and confident look about him. The bus conductor made his way to the man and asked, "Where are you headed?"

With a small, knowing smile, the man answered, "Jaisalmer." His voice was filled with a sense of purpose, as if he was heading exactly where he needed to be.

Chapter 9

Sherkhan

At the busy Jaisalmer bus stand, the morning was filled with the usual noise and activity. Around 11:00 AM, amidst the hustle, Lalu Singh got off the bus. He looked around with keen eyes, stretching away the stiffness of the journey. Spotting a nearby tea stall.

Approaching the stall. The vendor, engrossed in his task, didn't look up but responded, "It'll be ready in 2 minutes. Have a seat inside."

Lalu Singh, with a friendly nod, found a stool inside and picked up a newspaper, immersing himself in the headlines. Moments later, the vendor, tea in hand, approached him. A flicker of unease crossed the vendor's face with fear and terror, realizing he was no one but Lalu Singh in front of him.

"Your tea, Hukum," the vendor offered the cup with a shaky hand.

Lalu Singh, absorbed in an article, replied without looking up, "Just place it beside me, thank you."

Finishing his tea, Lalu Singh savored its unique taste. He reached into his wallet and asked, "What do I owe you?"

The vendor, now visibly anxious, folded his hands. "How can I take money from you, Sir? Your visit is lucky for me."

Lalu Singh, noticing the vendor's unease, firmly placed a 100-rupee note down, despite any protest. As he left, murmurs and hushed conversations broke out among the other shopkeepers. One whispered, "Was that Lalu Singh?" Another shopkeeper looked on curiously, asking, "Why's he back after all this time?" A third voiced his concern, "They say Lalu Singh only shows up when there's trouble brewing." The air was thick with anticipation, hinting that something significant was about to unfold.

Location: Empire Hotel, Jaisalmer

Time: 10:00 AM

The staff quietly set down a tray of breakfast, the aroma of freshly brewed coffee filling the air. In the adjacent room, young Mihir Kumar was lost in the world of cartoons, the TV casting flickering lights across his face.

In the midst of this tranquil scene, Jaswant Kumar lay in a deep sleep, oblivious to the world around him. His wife, Vaishali Kumar, stood by the bed, a mix of concern and exasperation in her voice.

"Jaswant… Jaswant…" she called out gently at first, then with increasing urgency. "It's already 10. Breakfast is here. Come on, wake up. Aren't you supposed to be at the hotel today? Wake up, Jaswant."

From the depths of his slumber, Jaswant mumbled a response, barely audible. "Hmm… just 2 more minutes."

Vaishali's tone shifted to one of frustration. "Hey!!! Jaswant, wake up!"

At that moment, Vaishali called out to Mihir for breakfast. The young boy emerged from his cartoon trance, a look of surprise on his face as he saw his father still in bed.

"Dad is still sleeping!" he exclaimed.

"Yes, I've never seen him sleep like this before. It's as if he has forgotten all his responsibilities. He's sleeping like there's no work waiting for him."

Location: R.L. Memorial Hospital, Jaisalmer

Time: 10:00 AM

Bindu sat anxiously in front of the doctor, who was meticulously reviewing medical reports.

"Is Mister Pokhar your father?" the doctor inquired, looking up from the reports.

"Yes, doctor. How's he now?"

"He's stable and has regained consciousness. He's ready to be discharged," the doctor reassured Bindu.

Bindu sighed in relief. "Thank you, doctor."

The doctor continued, "However, there are serious concerns. Due to ANS, your father is facing critical cardiac problems. He's had minor strokes before, leading to partial paralysis. This is his second such attack, and I must warn you, a third could be fatal. Has he been regularly taking his medication?"

Bindu: "Yes, I've been overseeing it."

The doctor sighed, "The medication is designed to thin the blood for easier heart access. But the recent attack was caused by a thick blood clot, indicating irregular medication. Consistent medication could have prevented this. I'm prescribing new medicines now, and it's crucial he takes them without fail."

Bindu listened intently, understanding the gravity of the situation. "I'll make sure he follows the prescription closely."

Location: District Jail, Jaisalmer

Time: 11:30 AM (Morning)

In the somber darkness of his cell, Kalu Singh sat, his fingers tracing old scars on the wall, each a silent testament to his time in confinement. The sudden clang of the cell door echoed through the gloom as a constable entered, a bundle of clothes in hand.

"Get dressed. You're out on bail, hukum," he announced.

Kalu Singh, his eyes narrowing suspiciously, questioned, "Who's playing the savior?"

"Pappu," the constable replied dryly.

"Pappu?" Kalu Singh chuckled darkly. "The little puppet pulling strings now, huh?"

After coming out of the cell, Kalu Singh stands in front of the Sub-Inspector. The Sub-Inspector is sitting on a stool, writing in a diary.

Kalu Singh: "I was transferred from Jodhpur to Jaisalmer. What suddenly happened yesterday?"

Sub-Inspector: "Even I don't have that information, Hukum. Please sign here. You have to be here before midnight tonight."

Kalu Singh: (Angry) "Are you instructing me what to do? I would tear you right now if you crossed the line."

As Kalu Singh stepped out of the jail's dim confines, Pappu was there with a car, offering a greeting, but Kalu Singh, just got into the back seat without a word. They drove off, the car's engine rumbling softly in the quiet.

"Who's behind my bail?"

"Sherkhan," Pappu replied.

"Suddenly?" Kalu Singh

There's something he needs to discuss," Pappu responded, steering the car onto Jethwai Road.

As they drove, the landscape grew increasingly desolate, heightening the sense of impending doom. "Where are we headed?"

"To a secret meeting with Sherkhan," Pappu.

"What kind of secret meeting?"

Pappu, maintaining his composure, remained tight-lipped. "Only Sherkhan knows,"

Upon reaching their destination, a barren and isolated spot, Pappu gestured toward the hills. "Sherkhan is waiting for you there"

Kalu Singh stepped out of the car. "What kind of secret meeting?" he repeated

Pappu: "I don't know, bhai. Sherkhan will explain."

They began ascending the sandy hills, Kalu Singh leading the way with Pappu trailing behind. The silence around them was oppressive, broken only by the sound of their footsteps on the sand. Halfway up, Kalu Singh stopped and turned, his senses heightened, aware that something significant, potentially dangerous, was about to unfold. Kalu Singh's instincts were on high alert, sensing the danger that was about to come.

"Give me your phone; I need to talk to Sherkhan,"

Pappu hesitated, fueling Kalu Singh's rising anger. "Don't test my patience, you son of a bitch."

Suddenly, a relaxed voice interrupted the tense scene.

"Look at my brother, unchanged from a decade ago, still with that fiery temper…" Lalu Singh remarked, an amused smile on his face.

Kalu Singh whirled around, his eyes narrowing at the sight of his brother. "You?" he spit out downward, looking at his younger brother in anger.

Lalu Singh, replied with a grin, "Missed you, brother. Didn't expect a warm welcome?"

Kalu Singh (shouting, veins pulsating with anger): "What the hell are you doing here, huh? Didn't Sherkhan make it crystal clear that you're banned from Jaisalmer for good? Are you deaf or just plain stupid? I knew you wouldn't give a damn about the rules. Thought you were smarter, but no, you're a complete idiot! You're testing my patience, and trust me, you don't want to see what happens when I lose it. Get out before I do something I'll enjoy way too much!"

Lalu Singh: "For a decade, I've kept my promise, never straying. Yet here you are, drawing me back with your stubborn ways. What unfolded 2 days ago was out of the ordinary. If you had simply asked, I would have returned. Why go through all this trouble?"

Kalu Singh's fury reached a boiling point, his voice dripping with sarcasm and disbelief. "Me? Accuse me, you fool?" he sneered. "Sitting in a cell while you roam free, and you lack the basic sense to see it?" He started laughing loudly, echoing with mockery and disdain.

The tension between them skyrocketed as Lalu Singh, with unnerving calmness, pulled out a gun and pointed it directly at Kalu Singh. "You shouldn't have done this."

"You want to kill me, yeah, common, go ahead, you bastard. (laughing hard) But remember Sherkhan, He will never forgive you, nor will I feel scared of you or death; I just feel how…"

Before he could utter another word, the air was split by the sound of gunfire. It wasn't Lalu Singh who had pulled the trigger, but an unseen assailant from behind. Time stretched into a surreal slow-motion as Kalu Singh felt the bullets rip into him. Each shot was like a fiery lance of pain, tearing through his flesh, sending shock waves of agony through his body. His knees buckled, and he collapsed into the sand, his laughter turning into a gurgle of blood. The desert around him seemed to stand still, a silent witness to his violent downfall.

Pappu, standing a distance away, wore a satisfied smile.

"Your aim is impressive," Lalu Singh complimented.

Pappu, beaming with pride, replied, "Thank you."

As Lalu Singh commanded Pappu to check Kalu Singh's pockets, the smirking assassin found nothing.

Lalu Singh:"Are you sure there's nothing in his pockets?"

Pappu – "No, checked 3 times."

Lalu Singh: (smiling) "Ok."

Location: Empire Hotel, Jaisalmer

Time: 01:00 PM

In the comfortable confines of their hotel room, Jaswant Kumar and his young son Mihir were engrossed in watching cartoons on TV.

Vaishali Kumar, entering the room, looked at her husband with a mix of amusement and disbelief. "What's this, Jaswant? Skipping the hotel today?"

Jaswant Kumar: "Today's a holiday, Vaishali. A day for relaxation. If I'm always at work, when will I have time for Mihir? So, no hotel today."

Vaishali raised an eyebrow, questioning his sudden change in attitude. "Leaving the hotel to others? That's quite trusting of you."

Jaswant Kumar: "A Day won't make much difference. It's good to be carefree sometimes."

Vaishali shook her head, a slight smile playing on her lips. "Impressive; I never knew you had it in you to be so carefree."

Leaving the room to go to the bathroom, Vaishali left father and son to their cartoons. Mihir, looking up at his dad, asked, "When will we go home, Dad?"

"Soon, Mihir. But first, let's see which gadget Doraemon is going to use now"

"Dad, Doraemon always has a gadget for every problem. I wish I had one."

As they continued watching, Mihir absentmindedly flipped the channel, landing on a news station. Jaswant's eyes narrowed, sensing something important. "Hold on, Mihir. Let's watch this for a couple of minutes."

Mihir groaned, "No, Dad, I don't like news."

"Just 2 minutes." Jaswant insisted, taking the remote and turning up the volume.

The news anchor's voice filled the room with a grave report: "Just now, we've received reports that 2 people have been found dead near the old Ring Road of Jaisalmer-Bikaner. The police have identified one of the deceased as Kalu Singh, a notorious criminal involved in the underworld and several serious crimes. The other victim, found close by, has been identified as Pappu, known to be an associate of Kalu Singh. The police suspect that a dispute between the 2 led to a fatal shootout. This incident has raised concerns about the current state of law and order in Jaisalmer."

Jaswant's expression turned a sign of relief as he listened to the news. A sense of urgency washed over him, and he abruptly stood up. "Vaishali, I need to go to the hotel," he called out with an excited tone.

Vaishali: "What happened? I can't hear you."

Without another word, Jaswant quickly got ready and hurried out.

Location: Old Jaisalmer–Bikaner Bypass

Time: 2:00 PM

A flurry of police activity had transformed the usually quiet area into a hub of investigation. Senior officers, technicians, and investigators huddled around tables laden with documents, photos, and maps, piecing together the events of a shocking crime scene. The area was cordoned off, with heavy police presence maintaining a perimeter.

Off to the side, away from the main hustle, stood 2 police officers, deep in conversation, beside their patrol car.

They were in stark contrast to each other, yet united in their purpose. The first was Inspector Jaspal, a 44-year-old with a stout build and a fair complexion. His stance was relaxed yet alert, his eyes betraying years of experience that had shaped his somewhat cynical outlook on life. The second, Sub-Inspector Nathuram, was his younger counterpart, 38 years of age, with a medium build and a darker complexion. Jaspal, ever the cynic, was munching on nuts, his eyes scanning the scene with a mix of disinterest and weariness. "Something's brewing,"

Nathuram, idealistic, looked at him questioningly. "What do you mean, Sir?"

Jaspal: "Watch and learn. The DSP will put on a show for the media – big promises and bold statements. Then he'll ask us to keep the investigation on the back burner, label it as a personal dispute or a random shootout and close the case. That's the routine."

Nathuram sighed, "That's how it goes in our system, sadly."

Jaspal's gaze drifted back to the crowd. "Just looking at them gives me a headache. Let's head out."

As they settled into their car, with Nathuram at the wheel and Jaspal still snacking, Nathuram: "Sir, don't you think there's something odd about this case?"

Jaspal laughed, holding up a peanut. "You know what's odd? These tasteless nuts." His laughter, with a touch of carelessness.

Nathuram: "Though Pappu was just a small-time crook – snatching, brawling, petty theft. And Kalu Singh is a big fish with a notorious reputation. The 2 being involved in this… it doesn't add up."

Jaspal: "Exactly, Pappu was no match for Kalu Singh, It's hard to believe."

Jaspal gazed out of the car window, "Well, we might just have to dig deeper than what's on the surface. We'll keep our eyes and ears open. After all, truth has a way of coming out."

Location: 512, Gandhi Nagar, Jaisalmer

Time: 12:30 PM

An ambulance quietly left the Pokhar residence. Bindu sat near a pond, his emotions in turmoil, as he watched hospital staff help his father into their home.

Once his father was settled in bed, Bindu went inside to be with him. Worry was clear on his face. Despite his weariness, Pokhar tried to lighten the atmosphere. With a weak but spirited voice, he started a joke, "Once, an elephant proposed to an ant…" Bindu, his patience frayed, interrupted sharply. "Did you take your medicine regularly before?"

Ignoring the question, Pokhar continued with his joke. However, Bindu, visibly emotional, insisted, "Tell me, did you take your medicine or not?"

Pokhar: "I did." Yet, his son, knowing his father's tendencies, saw through the facade.

"How could you be so careless?" Bindu's voice rose, "I've told you time and again how important your medication is. You can't ignore your health like this."

Pokhar: "Son, you can't imagine my joy when you got your job. But then I saw how all your earnings were going into my medical expenses. I didn't want to be a financial burden on you."

Bindu: "Do you think I care about the money? You are my world, Dad. Without you, my life has no meaning. And to hear you talk about yourself as a burden…"

Pokhar, looking weary and sorry, could only give a weak apology. "I'm sorry; what else can an old man say?"

Bindu couldn't be comforted. His voice cracked as he talked about all he had done for his father's care, his fear of losing him, and the hard times he had gone through.

Feeling too much from the talk, Bindu rushed out of the house and slammed the door behind him.

Location: The Titan Hotel

Time: 5:00 PM

Jaswant Kumar stood in the quiet lobby of The Titan Hotel, phone in hand, a look of determination mixed with anxiety on his face. He dialed a number, his fingers hesitating slightly before making the call.

"Hello… Hi Jennifer, I need to talk to you. Is this the right time?"

"No," came Jennifer's crisp reply, her tone indicating she was not in the mood for a conversation.

Jaswant rushed to speak before she could hang up. "Wait, please. I understand, Jennifer, and I am truly sorry for what happened. It was an accident, and I take full responsibility. I never meant to harm anyone."

Jennifer: "So?"

"I've made mistakes, but I've learned from them. I assure you, nothing like that will happen again. I've taken every precaution for our staff's safety. Please, give me another chance. Will you visit Titan Hotel…

Before he could finish, Jennifer interrupted, "I'm in the middle of a job interview, Mr. Kumar. You should find someone else."

Desperate, Jaswant blurted out, "I want you to take charge of Titan Hotel. There's no one else as capable as you."

The line went dead.

Jaswant, undeterred, dialed another number. "Hi Pushpa, I am Jaswant Kumar."

Pushpa's voice was warm. "Hi Sir, how are you? I was about to call you about Reena."

Jaswant Kumar: "Pushpa, listen carefully. I've decided to reopen the hotel, and I need you to come back."

He then proceeded to make a series of calls, contacting staff members, Govardhan Singh and Bhopat, each conversation echoing his determination to revive The Titan Hotel.

After some calculating thought process:

Jaswant Kumar: "Hi, this is Jaswant Kumar."

Rinku's voice was filled with surprise and happiness. "Oh, hi, Sir! I'm so glad you called. Today was tough, but your call…"

Jaswant, cutting him off, got straight to the point. "Rinku, we're reopening the hotel, and I want you back at work."

Rinku's excitement was palpable. "Really, Sir? Thank you! I…"

Jaswant Kumar: "Be at the hotel tomorrow at 12 PM."

Hanging up, Jaswant stood alone in the silent lobby, his resolve firm. The Titan Hotel, his dream and passion, would not succumb to adversity. It was time to turn a new page, to start anew.

Location: 512, Gandhi Nagar, Jaisalmer

Time: 07:00 PM

As the evening light dimmed, the peace in Pokhar's room was broken. The door creaked open, waking Pokhar from his uneasy sleep. "Bindu?" he called out weakly but got no answer.

Before Pokhar could react further, 2 men entered the room.

At 33, Joseph's medium build and dark complexion gave him an imposing presence. Alongside him was Mangu, a 26-year-old with a fair complexion and a medium build.

Joseph: "How are you feeling now?" he asked, his voice calm but firm.

Pokhar: "Who are you?"

Mangu: "We're friends of Bindu."

Pokhar: "Bindu didn't tell me about you, and he's not here."

Joseph: "That's okay. He doesn't need to be here for this."

Things started to feel more threatening when Joseph took out a small bottle and a syringe from his jacket. Pokhar's fear grew. "Bindu should be back soon…" he said, his voice full of worry.

"Don't be scared. It's going to be okay," Joseph said, as he filled the syringe with liquid from the bottle and walked over to Pokhar.

Pokhar knew something bad was happening, but he couldn't do anything. Joseph held his arm and injected him. "Just a second," Joseph said softly as he put the needle into Pokhar's skin.

Location: 512, Gandhi Nagar, Jaisalmer

Time: 08:00 PM

Bindu returned home in the evening with a new wheelchair, hoping to surprise his father. He found the front door slightly open, an unusual and worrying sight.

"Father? Did someone visit?" he called out, stepping into the disheveled living room. "Papa… Papa? Are you upset with me? "I brought something special for you. You won't be confined to this room anymore!" He announces cheerfully, but his voice trails off as he notices the unsettling silence.

Rushing into the bedroom, a harrowing sight stops him cold. His father, Pokhar, lies motionless, his eyes shut, with a disturbing froth at his mouth. Near the bed, a sinister-looking bottle and syringe tell a story of their own. Moving toward his father in panic, as if every step was overpowering him. There was fear on his face, and whole body started trembling. A wave of panic and shock washed over Bindu as he discovered an envelope which contained a message: "If the money isn't delivered, you'll be the next to fall."

Chapter 10

This is Business

Location: The Cremation Ground, Jaisalmer

Time: 6:00 AM

Dawn had barely broken when Bindu, shrouded in grief, performed the last rites for his father. A hushed silence enveloped the cremation ground, broken only by the solemn chants of a nearby priest completing the ritualistic ceremonies. As the final rites concluded, Bindu's tears were unmistakable, his sorrow a tangible presence in the cool morning air. He retreated to a corner, his figure a portrait of loss and despair.

The priest, a kind-eyed man draped in white, approached Bindu with a comforting presence. "Don't be disheartened, my child. Everything will be fine," he murmured, his voice a soothing balm.

Bindu looked up, his voice choked with emotion. "Your fee?"

"2000," replied the priest gently.

The scene shifted to Jaswant, who, with his family, was leaving the sanctuary of the Empire Hotel. They were packed into the car, embarking on the journey home.

Vaishali: "Can we be sure that nothing like this will happen again?"

"If something like that were to happen, we would have stayed at the hotel. Trust me, nothing like that will happen again"

Place: 7B, Shastri Nagar, Jaisalmer

Time 9:00 AM

Upon their arrival near their house, an unexpected figure approached. It was Phoolan Devi, her expression one of startled recognition.

"Oh, Vaishali, I thought…" she began, but before she could finish, Jaswant, sensing a threat in her presence — the danger of her spilling everything — hastily interjected.

"Phoolanji, we have some work. Let's discuss it later," he said, his voice sharp, a clear note of urgency cutting through.

Phoolan Devi, taken aback by his abruptness, tried to continue, "But I was just asking…"

"Not now," Jaswant cut in firmly, his demeanor brooking no argument. "Unload the luggage; it's getting late," he directed, effectively steering Vaishali away from Phoolan Devi, who, still bewildered, reluctantly left the scene.

"What was that about?" Vaishali, "You shouldn't have spoken like that, especially to an elder."

"We have more work, Vaishali, and I know her habit of non-stop chattering,"

Jaswant made a call to Kaishav Jain, his tone impatient. "We are waiting outside the house, and your man hasn't arrived yet to open the lock."

"He will come. Learn to be patient; there's always a story behind every success," came the calm response from Kaishav Jain before the call ended.

As Vaishali unloaded the luggage, she noticed scratches on the car, her concern evident. "Jaswant, how did these scratches get here?" she inquired.

"You know, there was a collision that day?" Jaswant replied, evasive.

"But Bhati Circle is a one-sided road. The scratches should be on the opposite side," Vaishali countered, her suspicion grows.

Jaswant Kumar: "You're overthinking this, Vaishali. Not every doubt has a clear answer."

"You're hiding something from me, Jaswant. What are you up to?" Vaishali.

"I am not hiding anything. I am your husband, not an enemy," Jaswant retorted, his voice tinged with frustration.

Location: Seven Lodge Nagar

Time: 9:30 AM

Bindu was hiding, watching Don Robert's house closely. After some time, he tucked a knife into his pocket and started walking toward the house. When he got close, he saw guards in front of the house. They wouldn't let him in.

Trying to get past them, but the guards were too strong. They pushed him back hard, and he fell onto the road.

The main guard looked down at him. "You should leave now. Don't make us force you," he said, clearly warning Bindu.

Location: The Titan Hotel

Time: 12:00 PM

Jaswant Kumar walked into The Titan Hotel and sat down at a table, looking like he was waiting for someone. Soon, Rinku drove up in a car. Jaswant went outside.

"Hi Sir, so good to see you after a long time," Rinku greeted him.

"Me too, come inside," Jaswant replied

Inside, Rinku said, "Sir, this place hasn't changed. I remember when Reena was shot here…" Suddenly, Jaswant pulled out a gun and pointed it at him.

Rinku, scared and raising his hands, asked, "What's wrong, Sir? Did I do something wrong?"

"You made a big mistake. You thought I was just a simple, easy-to-trick businessman, right? But you're wrong. Do you know who I am? I was behind your boss Kalu Singh's death. I got him out of my way, and now you're next," Jaswant said firmly.

Rinku, very nervous, replied, "Sir, it's not my fault. I was just following orders."

"What orders?" Jaswant asked.

"Everything I did, I did on Kalu Singh ji's orders. I was just a kid picking up trash, barely noticed by anyone. Then, one day, Kalu Singh ji himself approached me. He looked at me and asked, 'Will you work for me?' That moment changed everything. I pledged my loyalty to him. He was the one who placed me in the Hayat Hotel. It was under his command that I disabled those cameras."

"And then what did Kalu Singh do?" Jaswant asked.

"He shot that girl," Rinku said.

Jaswant then warned him, "Well, thanks for unfolding. All our talks were recorded on a hidden camera. From now on, you work for me. If you think of making a mistake a second time, I'll give these recordings to the police. Got it?"

"Yes, Sir, I'll do whatever you say. Please don't shoot," Rinku pleaded.

Jaswant threw the gun at Rinku and said, "This is fake."

Location: Rasesar Colony, Jaisalmer

Time: 12:00 PM

In the small but warm kitchen of their Rasesar Colony home, Shantidevi, a 35-year-old dedicated wife and mother, was busy cooking. The aroma of spices filled the air. Nearby, her husband, Jaspal, was deeply engaged in conversation with their 15-year-old daughter, Khushi. Despite her physical disability that kept her bound to a wheelchair, Khushi's spirit was unbreakable.

As Shantidevi stirred the pot, she glanced over her shoulder. "Don't you have to go to the police station?" she asked Jaspal, her voice tinged with concern.

Jaspal, slightly irritated, replied without looking away from Khushi. "Shanti, how many times have I told you not to disturb me when I am with Khushi?"

Khushi, looking up from her books, added gently, "Papa, I will study, you go, you're getting late."

"No, son, you are more important to me than duty. Now tell me, what is the value of alpha plus minus Y?" Jaspal asked, turning back to her studies.

"Minus alpha without bracket," Khushi replied confidently.

Jaspal beamed with pride. "Well done, Shanti, I am telling you, our Khushi will make a name in the world one day."

Khushi, hesitating slightly, voiced a deeper concern. "Dad, can I ask you something? I can't walk. In school, everyone says, 'What will you do even if you come first?' and laughs."

Jaspal paused, then spoke with a comforting tone. "OK, let me tell you a story. There was a person. He couldn't walk like you, couldn't speak, couldn't hear. But today, the world considers him the greatest person ever born on this planet. With his abilities, he forced the world to take pride in him. Fighting his physical limitations, he achieved everything that people can only imagine. Do you know his name?Dr. Stephen Hawking. Remember, a person is disabled or mentally handicapped by his mind, not by the body. So, never consider yourself sick. Now tell me, is your school open?"

Khushi nodded, "Yes, why, Papa?"

Location: Holy Convent School, Jaisalmer

Time: 01:00 PM

Jaspal takes his daughter to school, into her class, where teaching is in progress, and the teacher is instructing the children.

Jaspal: "Excuse me. I apologize for disturbing all of you during the class."

Teacher: "Who are you? Khushi, who is he? No one can enter the class without permission."

Jaspal takes out his Inspector ID from his pocket and shows it to the teacher.

Jaspal (looking toward the children): "I am Khushi's father. Normally, I shouldn't be here, but if anyone mistreats my daughter, I will come back, even if it's the second time. And now I am explaining it with love. I want all the children to listen carefully because I won't come to explain it the second time. My daughter is my world, and it won't be good if anyone messes with my world."

Location: The Titan Hotel

Time: 1:00 PM

The gates of The Titan Hotel were wide open as a van smoothly rolled in. Jaswant Kumar, standing nearby, watched it closely.

"The van has arrived. They came straight here, didn't stop anywhere, right?"(On Phone) Jaswant asked, his eyes not leaving the van.

Kaishav Jain, with a hint of pride in his voice, replied, "Mr. Kumar, you know my work is always perfect. Everything happened just as you said."

As Jaswant stepped outside, the van's doors opened. Pushpa, Bhopat and Govardhan stepped out, followed by Jennifer, who emerged last. Jaswant's face lit up with surprise and happiness at the sight of Jennifer.

"Welcome back. It's great to see all of you again," he greeted them warmly.

"Sir, where is Reena, Ma'am?" Pushpa inquired with concern.

"She's still in the hospital, but she'll be back soon," Jaswant replied, then turned to Govardhan and Bhopat. "How are you both?"

"Sir, everything is fine," Govardhan responded with a nod.

Jaswant then approached Jennifer. "Thank you for coming,"

Jennifer, however, remained silent, offering no response.

Jaswant, addressing everyone, said, "Now, please go to your rooms, leave your bags, and then come to the hall. I have something important to tell all of you."

After a while, the staff gathered in the hall, with Jaswant Kumar standing before them.

"I want to share a story with you," he began, his voice carrying across the hall. "It's about a farmer from a small village in Madhya Pradesh who had dreams bigger than his circumstances. He could have lived a simple life like any other farmer, but he thought differently. He sold his land and moved to Mumbai, where he started a small steel factory. He faced many failures, but never lost hope. He took loans and faced struggles but kept his eyes on his goal. He worked tirelessly until he achieved what he dreamed of."

"Today, his company makes 200 billion annually. Yes, 200 billion! And let me reveal something – he is none other than my father, Prithviraj Kumar. I am his son, the inheritor of an empire. I could have just followed in his footsteps and worked there, but I chose to create my own legacy. I came here with a goal as ambitious as the one my father had 40 years ago. And now, here I stand, having realized my dream – this magnificent hotel, a symbol of determination and excellence."

Jaswant's eyes swept across the hall, meeting those of his staff. "And now, I want you all to embrace this vision, the way my father once did. We are a team, and together, we must strive to reach new heights, to achieve our dreams. This is our time, our struggle, and I promise, our success is inevitable. Yes, what happened recently was unfortunate. But if we let that incident break our spirit today, then we haven't really achieved anything."

He paused for a moment, letting his words sink in. "It's time to leave the past behind and start anew. We'll face challenges, but we must do it together. This is the essence of business; this is business, the path to success. We will make our shared dream a reality! And we will prove it to the world. Are you all with me?"

The room was filled with renewed energy, a sense of unity, and purpose. Jaswant's words had not just conveyed his story; they had ignited a collective ambition, a shared determination to overcome and succeed. "Are you all with me?"

The hall echoed with the unified response of the staff. "Yes, Sir!" they chorused, their voices blending into a powerful affirmation of their commitment and unity.

Jaswant Kumar, feeling the energy in the hall, encouraged them to express their enthusiasm even more. "And louder!" he called out, his voice ringing with leadership and conviction.

In response, the staff raised their voices, their collective spirit and resolve resonating through the hall. "Yes, Sir!" they exclaimed, louder and more confidently. The words were not just a reply; they were a declaration of their readiness to face challenges and work together toward a common goal.

Location: Titan Hotel

Time: 3:00 PM

Bindu burst into The Titan Hotel, his face a mask of grief and fear. He found Jaswant Kumar and, unable to contain his emotions, broke down in front of him.

Jaswant, taken aback, quickly asked, "What happened?"

Bindu, tears streaming down his face, couldn't find the words to speak.

Jaswant urged him gently, "Bindu… Bindu, stop crying; tell me what happened."

Through his sobs, Bindu managed to speak. "That Robert killed my father while I was begging for money. It's all your fault. Why did he have to hurt my father? He was everything I ever had. And today, he's no more. My life has been scattered. I don't understand what to do and what not to do; I am left alone."

Jaswant, moved by his distress, embraced Bindu, trying to offer some comfort. "Who said you are alone? I am with you. Don't worry and calm down."

Bindu, still crying, feared for his own life. "He will kill me too."

"That won't happen," Jaswant assured him.

Bindu, desperate, pleaded, "Do something... It's all because of you. You promised nothing would happen to me."

Jaswant thought for a moment before speaking. "Bindu, you'll have to hide for a few days."

Confused, Bindu asked, "What do you mean? Where?"

Jaswant explained, "The place you thought of, remember? There are underground rooms. You'll stay there for a while."

Bindu panicked and refused. "No, I won't stay there. Why don't you give me the money?"

Jaswant shook his head. "Don't you get it? I don't have a penny right now. This is the only way. If you want to stay alive, stay underground while I work on a solution."

Jaswant then led Bindu discreetly to the underground area. "There are plenty of rooms; pick any. I'll take care of food and drinks. Don't come out for any reason," he instructed firmly.

Bindu, still upset, persisted. "Just give me the money."

Jaswant, a bit exasperated, replied, "You're not understanding. I don't have any money right now. This is the only safe option for you. Stay here, and I'll find a way to fix this. Just remember, don't come out under any circumstances."

Location: The Titan Hotel

Time: 06:00 PM

Inside the hotel, all the staff was gathered together, preparing for a new beginning. Each staff member was dedicated to reviving the hotel's sparkle. The scent of shining white linens and the fragrance of scattered hopes filled the rooms. The staff was not only involved in preparing the immaculate hotel but were also inspired to reach new heights themselves.

A stage filled with determination was leading them toward a new beginning. Everyone understood that through these cleaning efforts, the hotel could be revived; Rinku was cleaning the hotel's board. Jaswant

Kumar was watching from below, where, once again, the board of Titan Hotel was shining. Seeing this, Jaswant Kumar felt proud that he had finally started the hotel again. Finally, overcoming all the troubles, he had achieved victory. But Jaswant Kumar was unaware that he hadn't rid himself of troubles but had rather extended an invitation to challenges that would change history.

Chapter 11

Light, Camera, Action...

Location: 7B, Shastri Nagar, Jaisalmer

Time: 8:00 AM

Jaswant Kumar was on the phone, his tone serious. "I need a professional team. It has to be perfect."

"Don't worry," came Kaishav Jain's confident voice from the other end. "The city's best team will be on it."

"And what about after everything is set?" Jaswant probed further.

"Telecast, paper ads, and all that. We'll handle everything. Just keep in mind, the cost can be tough," Kaishav replied.

"I've got that covered," Jaswant assured.

Ending the call, Jaswant turned to leave the house. "I'm off to the hotel," he announced.

Vaishali, concerned, called out to him, "Oh, have breakfast before you go."

Jaswant, checking his watch, replied briskly, "Not today, I'm running late."

Location: The Titan Hotel

Time: 12:00 PM

In the dimly lit underground area of The Titan Hotel, Bindu sat alone, his stomach growling with hunger. The long wait was wearing on him, and finally, unable to resist any longer, he decided to emerge.

As he ascended from the underground, Jennifer spotted him unexpectedly.

"What brings you here?"

Bindu, caught off guard, stammered, "Just casually; I mean, I was here earlier in the morning."

Jennifer, her gaze fixed on him, pressed further. "So, what's your reason for being here now?"

Bindu fell silent, unable to find a convincing answer.

Location: Jaisalmer Police Station

Time: 10:00 AM

Jaspal was in the middle of a light-hearted moment with his fellow officers at the Jaisalmer Police Station. He was

recounting a funny incident from his time in Patiala. "…
It's about Patiala. I told the head officer that we'd caught
a truck full of liquor… and you know what he said?
'Wow, now catch 2 more trucks for soda and snacks…'"

The officers around him burst into laughter, enjoying the
humorous break in their routine. Just then, Nathuram
called out to Jaspal. "Sir, are you coming here?"

Jaspal, with a smile still lingering on his face, turned
to his colleagues. "Enough of this enjoyable banter,
everyone. Let's get back to work."

Nathuram was intently watching the camera footage
on the computer, looking for any evidence. "Sir, I
checked the entire day's recording, and except for the
car carrying Kalu Singh, no other vehicle went through
the intersection that day."

Jaspal, still in a light mood, called out to another officer.
"Mukesh, bring tea and biscuits. And yes, some chickpeas,
too. There's something special about chickpeas." He then
turned back to Nathuram. "Yes, what were you saying?"

Nathuram tried to continue, "Sir, I was saying…"

But Jaspal interrupted him again with a sudden thought.
"Tell me, how many roads are near the bypass? There

must be another way to get onto that road. Check all the cameras around there."

Location: The Titan Hotel

Time: 1:00 PM

Jaswant Kumar rushed into The Titan Hotel, quickly grabbing a lunchbox before heading to the underground area. When he got there, he noticed that Bindu was already eating.

"Who gave you the food?" Jaswant asked, a hint of concern in his voice.

Bindu, clearly irritated, shot back, "You locked me down here, and I was starving since morning."

Jaswant's concern turned to anger. "I'm asking you again: who gave you the food?"

"Jennifer did, idiot," Bindu retorted. "If I had been waiting for you, I would have died of hunger by now."

Jaswant's anger intensified. "I told you not to come out. You can't trust anyone here. Someone might find out where you're hiding. This simple formula, you just don't get it, do you?"

Location: The Titan Hotel

Time: 1:30 PM

Jaswant found Jennifer and approached her. "I'm the one who kept Bindu underground. His life is in danger, so…"

Jennifer cut him off. "When I first met you, I thought you were brave. But now, I see. Burning Reena, hiding all this, even an underground room in this hotel. What else are you keeping from us?"

Jaswant tried to explain. "I didn't think I needed to tell everyone about the underground. I swear I didn't plan all this. Please, Jennifer, keep Bindu being underground a secret. And could you take care of his food and water? I trust no one here but you. He's in danger, and this needs to stay between us."

Jennifer: "Tell me one thing, that day when Reena was facing death, and you turned a car on a dirt road, was it intentional? Because as far as I know, there is no shortcut to go to Jaisalmer. Everyone knows this. That means you had already planned to burn her."

Jaswant's face remained silent upon hearing this. Seeing this, Jennifer left from there angrily.

As Jaswant Kumar was inside The Titan Hotel, Pushpa called out to him from outside.

"A call came from Reena's house. They were asking about her, and they're coming here tomorrow," Pushpa said, her voice tinged with urgency.

Jaswant's face clouded with worry. "What did you tell them?"

Pushpa replied, "I didn't know what to say, so I hung up. But they said they're coming tomorrow. And yes, I wanted to ask one more thing… there are potholes on the walls in some places. Why so? Because these potholes weren't there when we left."

Jaswant Kumar (hurried): "I will explain it to you later. Ok."

Frustrated and distressed, Jaswant immediately goes outside the hotel and calls Kaishav Jain.

Jaswant: "Everything is messed up; we are in trouble."

Kaishav Jain: "I am at the construction site and have work…"

Jaswant: (interrupting) "Forget about your work; you need to help me. Reena's family is coming tomorrow."

Kaishav Jain: "Oh God, I'm not your servant. I haven't taken a contract every time, understand?"

Jaswant: "If I get into trouble, you won't survive either, Hoshiyarchand."

Kaishav Jain: "This was the only option left. I've never seen a person like you in my entire career."

Jaswant: "We need to do something, or everything will be ruined."

Kaishav Jain: "I need 60%, understand."

Jaswant: "Take it, you've already crossed the limit of greed. Now think, use your brain."

Kaishav Jain: "I'm not God; give me time to think. And if you use the word greedy again…"

Jaswant hangs up the phone.

Meanwhile, an advertising team arrived at the hotel for a promotional shoot. They began setting up their equipment. The director approached Jaswant with a problem.

"How's the arrangement?" Jaswant asked, surveying the setup.

"Jain Sir arranged it; it's top-notch. But we're missing an actor," the director informed him.

"What? After all this, no actor?" Jaswant was incredulous.

"The actor we booked is celebrating his birthday, and we can't find a replacement on such short notice in Jaisalmer," the director explained.

Jaswant Kumar: "So?"

Director: "I think you could be a good choice."

"So now I have to act? I've never done this before," Jaswant protested.

The director tried to reassure him. "You'll be fine. Just follow my lead. It's easy."

Soon, Jaswant was dressed in a coat, a script in hand. The director positioned him in front of the camera.

"Recite what is written in the script. When I say action, just narrate it. Ready? Light, camera, and action!"

Location: Jaisalmer Police Station

Time: 3:00 PM

Inside the quiet precincts of the Jaisalmer Police Station, Jaspal and Nathuram were intently studying the camera footage from various intersections. Their focus was unwavering, searching for any clue that might break the case wide open.

Suddenly, Nathuram's eyes narrowed as he spotted something unusual. "Sir, there's one place that looks suspicious. A truck stops, and a man gets out and heads toward the desert."

Jaspal, intrigued, leaned in closer. "Zoom in on that; I want a good look at his face."

Nathuram quickly adjusted the camera footage, zooming in on the figure emerging from the truck. As the image became clearer, his expression turned to one of shock.

"Sir, that's Lalu Singh!" Nathuram exclaimed, hardly believing what he was seeing.

A slow smile spread across Jaspal's face as he leaned back in his chair. "Finally, we've got him. The fish has taken the bait."

The room was filled with a sense of accomplishment as they realized they were one step closer to unraveling the mystery that had been eluding them.

Location: The Titan Hotel

Time: 7:00 PM

The evening had settled over The Titan Hotel with a deceptive calm. After the advertising shoot, the crew packed up and left, leaving the hotel in a quiet lull. But this tranquility was abruptly shattered when Jaswant Kumar heard the sound of breaking glass from an upper room. His heart pounding, he rushed to the source of the disturbance.

Upon reaching the room, Jaswant's worst fears materialized. Standing before him was Aslam, his face twisted with rage, a gun in his hand pointing toward him.

Jaswant, his voice trembling with fear, pleaded, "Please don't shoot; I haven't done anything to harm you. We can talk this out peacefully..."

"You ruined my life. I've been on the run day and night because of you. First, I'll shoot you, then..." Aslam's voice was cold and filled with vengeance.

"Wait, don't shoot. Let me explain. Killing me won't help you..." Jaswant stammered, desperately trying to reason with him.

Aslam, momentarily pausing, pulled out a video recorder from his pocket. "Fine, I'll give you one last chance to speak."

He started recording. "Now, confess everything. If you lie, I won't hesitate to pull the trigger."

Jaswant, beads of sweat forming on his forehead, started to confess. "Okay, I'll tell you. I took a trip to Hanumangarh, with a calculated plan in mind. I quietly placed a fake Aadhaar card of you, bearing your name, near Lalu Singh's factory. Then, I orchestrated a bomb explosion, a move designed to turn Lalu Singh's suspicions toward Kalu Singh and you. It was a strategic play, aimed at putting them against each other."

Aslam's grip on the gun tightened. "Good, now brace yourself for the bullet."

Jaswant, in a last-ditch effort to save himself, hurriedly said, "Wait, hear me out. I know you plan to show this to Lalu Singh, but do you really think he'll let you live? Do you honestly believe Lalu Singh, a man notorious for erasing his tracks, will spare you? He's the kind who leaves no trace, no evidence for the police. Remember what happened to Kalu Singh and Pappu? I won't let you get hurt; trust me. Just give me one last chance…"

Aslam's face hardened. "Shut up, scoundrel. You're more cunning than I ever imagined."

Jaswant, steadying his voice despite the evident fear, spoke with conviction, "Think about it – going to him is signing your own death warrant. He won't let you walk away alive. Trust me on this. All I ask is for one more chance to set things right. Listen, I won't let anything happen to you. Trust me. Just give me one last chance..."

Aslam, his curiosity piqued despite his anger, asked, "And what is that?"

Jaswant Kumar: "I have a plan."

Chapter 12

Khamma Ghanni

In the early morning light of Manesar, an elderly man and a woman emerged from a desert house, each carrying bags. They boarded a waiting jeep. The man asked the driver, "How many hours until we reach?"

"Approximately 6 hours." the driver responded.

As the jeep set off, leaving a trail of dust behind, the man and woman shared a look of mutual understanding, embarking on a significant journey across the vast, mysterious desert toward Jaisalmer.

Location: Pioneer Mall, Jaisalmer

Time: 10:00 AM

In the bustling atmosphere of Pioneer Mall, Jaspal was immersed in a fun-filled game with his daughter, Khushi. Their laughter echoed in the busy corridors, blending with the cheerful ambiance of the mall.

"How about having ice cream now?" Jaspal suggested, his eyes twinkling with mischief.

"Dad, why are you spending so much?" Khushi asked.

Jaspal replied with a wide grin, "I earn for you, my dear." Turning to the ice cream vendor, he ordered, "Give a vanilla."

As they waited for their ice cream, Jaspal's attention was drawn to a large advertisement screen showcasing a promo for The Titan Hotel. The ad painted a serene picture of the hotel, describing it as 'heaven on earth.'

[The camera pans over a majestic-looking hotel]

Jaswant Kumar: "Here, it's not just about beds and walls. It's about feeling at home, wrapped in warmth. Imagine the warmest hug from your grandmother – that's us!"

"Welcome to the, uh, Tighten… no, Titan Hotel! In the hearty heart of Rajasthan, where luxury meets… luxury!"

[The camera pans over the opulent lobby]

"Here, we have beds… and wall. But these aren't just any beds and walls! They're, um, very comfortable and… vertical. Yes, they definitely stand-up straight!"

"Behold the view! It's not just a view; it's a… viewing experience. Every day, it changes. Like, sometimes there's more sun, and sometimes less. Amazing, right?"

[The camera reveals a stunning landscape visible from the hotel.]

"Escape the busy world to this quiet… quiet place. So quiet, you can hear your own thoughts. Sometimes, it's too-quiet. Maybe bring a radio."

"Come to The Titan Hotel, where every stay is… um, a stay to remember. Yes, that sounds right! Don't believe us, just come and explore, because it is more than a hotel, this is heaven.")

Jaspal couldn't help but chuckle. "So quiet, you need a radio? What the hell? I didn't know there was such a recession going on that people had to pay for advertisements on local TV channels. And forget about the money; they could have at least hired a decent actor. "Look at this man," he joked to the ice cream vendor. "Hey, why don't you put your ice cream stall up there on the big screen? 'Ice cream so cold, it'll freeze your thoughts. Perfect for The Titan Hotel's too-quiet rooms!'"

His voice trailed off as he burst into another round of laughter, shaking his head in amusement. The ice cream vendor, catching on to the humor, joined in with a hearty chuckle. Khushi looked on, her face lit up with a smile, enjoying her father's humorous take on the advertisement.

Location: The Titan Hotel

Time: 11:00 AM

Jaswant Kumar, his face etched with worry, was on the phone in a quiet corner of The Titan Hotel. "Yes, this is Jaswant Kumar from Titan Hotel. Is the conversation with Reena's family ongoing? Listen, please stay calm. Reena had a bad fall down the stairs yesterday. She suffered a serious head injury and is now in the ICU at Nayak Hospital. But I assure you, everything will be fine. Please head directly to Nayak Hospital, where she's admitted."

The atmosphere in one of the hotel rooms was thick with unease. Aslam stood rigidly, his eyes dark with impending doom. Jaswant entered the room, trying to mask his own fear with a veneer of hospitality.

"If you need anything, let me know. Everything in the room is top-notch, like the TV, fridge, and…"

Aslam cut him off abruptly, "I'm leaving this evening."

Jaswant Kumar: "Where? Leaving from here is like calling death upon yourself."

Aslam: "You've already beckoned death. Do you think hiding me will save you? That's just wishful thinking. Lalu Singh is a monster, a terror to everyone. Your mistake has put not just me, but you, your family, and all of Jaisalmer in peril. I'll run, but where will you hide? He won't stop until he finds out who's responsible. He's coming for all of us…"

Jaswant, his voice strained, asked, "Where will you go?"

Aslam's response was resigned yet defiant. "To my home, Rawalpindi, in Pakistan."

"Without a passport?" Jaswant's question hung in the air.

Aslam's face hardened. "There are many underground tunnels at the border. I've found one for my escape."

The room fell silent, the weight of their predicament hanging between them like a thick fog, suffocating and inescapable.

Suddenly, Pushpa calls Jaswant from downstairs. Jaswant goes down and sees a person waiting near the counter.

Pushpa: "Sir, someone is here to meet you."

The person turns around, revealing himself as Lalu Singh. With that movement, Jaswant thought everything was finished… fear in his eyes filled with tension.

Lalu Singh (hugging Jaswant): "What a hotel you've made! Wow. This hotel is not just a hotel; it's heaven. Just as it was described on TV (laughs). Come on, let me become a fan of your craftsmanship."

Jaswant Kumar (nervously): "Thank you for your praise."

Lalu Singh: "Why not show me around the hotel? I'm excited to see all the rooms."

Jaswant Kumar shows Lalu Singh different rooms one by one.

Lalu Singh: "Wow! (with joy) Just wow! Praising the room is not enough; let me see all the hotel rooms."

Jaswant Kumar: "Hukum, Hotel has 166 rooms. It will take time."

Lalu Singh (smiling): "No problem. I'm enjoying this. Show me the rooms."

Jaswant Kumar shows one room after another. After a while, they reach the room where Aslam is hiding.

Jaswant Kumar: "Customers are staying here. If you disturb the guests…"

Lalu Singh: (interrupting): "So what? Show me the room."

Jaswant Kumar: "Guests will get disturbed, Hukum."

Lalu Singh (with a finger on his lips): "Shh… show me the room."

Jaswant Kumar knocked on the door, but there was no response. He knocked again, harder, but still nothing. "Maybe the guest is asleep," he said.

Lalu Singh stood next to him, staring at the door. "Break it down," he ordered,

Jaswant Kumar: "What!!"

"I said break it down," Lalu Singh said again with his calm tone.

Suddenly, Jaswant remembered something. "Wait, I have a spare key," he said quickly, his hands shaking as he searched his pockets.

Lalu Singh looked at him, "Then what's to worry about? Open it," he said, smiling.

Jaswant took out the key, his hands trembling as he tried to put it in the lock. The key clinked loudly against the door. He turned the key, his heart racing with fear and anticipation…

Jaswant Kumar hesitantly opens the door. Lalu Singh looks around.

A moment later, he stepped onto the balcony and noticed that the door to the next room's balcony was open. Chuckling at the sight, Lalu entered the adjoining room, followed by Jaswant. Lalu's attention was drawn to a wardrobe. As he approached, Nathuram's call interrupted.

Nathuram: "Hukum, this is Sub-Inspector Nathuram. Where are you?"

Suddenly, Jaspal snatched the phone.

Jaspal: "Wherever you are, stay there. We need some clarifications and investigations to conduct. Hope you'll fully cooperate."

Cutting the call, Lalu, smiling, grinning at the wardrobe, said, "Nice meeting you, Jaswant Kumar. We'll catch up soon. Perhaps, very soon."

Lalu Singh goes downstairs, glances at the tracker under his car, and drives away without removing it. Jaswant watches from the window. As soon as Lalu Singh leaves, Jaswant, drenched in sweat and gripped by fear, cautiously opens the wardrobe where Aslam had concealed himself, clenching a gun

Jaswant Kumar utters, "He knew you were here. However, suddenly, a phone call diverted his attention, forcing him to leave the place. Overall. That call saved your life. he's gone now."

Hearing this, with fear in his eyes, Aslam starts running away from there.

Jaswant Kumar: "Don't go out by mistake. This is only the safest place. Or otherwise, you won't survive…"

Aslam: "So, what should I do?"

Jaswant Kumar:"I have an underground hiding room…"

Aslam (interrupting): "Listen, you fool, a storm has come, and it won't spare anyone. Thanks to God that you are still alive; run away if you want to see yourself and your family alive."

Saying this, Aslam rushes away.

As the clock struck 1:30 in the afternoon on Jaisalmer Munabao Road, Nathuram, and Jaspal sat in the car heading toward The Titan Hotel. Jaspal, with a tracking device in his hand, pointed toward Lalu's car on display, depicting its proximity.

Jaspal: "A gesture was enough for the thief. Made a call, and he came running. But why is he coming? In spite of telling him to stop."

Nathuram: "How far is he indicating?"

Jaspal: "Not further. It seems like he's trapped in the net."

Nathuram: "If possible, let me talk to him."

Lalu's car pulled over in front of a police car. Lalu Singh, smiling, got out and embraced Nathuram.

Lalu Singh: "Nathuram, long time to see!"

Nathuram: "Ghanni khamma, hukum."

Lalu Singh: "Khamma Ghanni, it's nice to meet you after so many years. But Nathuram, when did you start doing this? Putting a tracker on my car without permission. Such a big mistake despite being a policeman."

Nathuram: "Sorry. Sir but…"

Jaspal: "I've fixed that tracker."

Lalu Singh: "Who is this gentleman?'

Nathuram: "Inspector Jaspal, shifted here just a year ago,"

Patting Jaspal's shoulder with a smile. Lalu Singh, grinning, greeted him, "Welcome to Jaisalmer."

Jaspal: (interrupting) "Remove your hand."

Lalu Singh: "What did you say?"

Jaspal: "I said move your hand. (To Nathuram) What is the reason for giving so much respect to this thug? (To Lalu) I am 44 years old, and for so many years, thousands of scoundrels like you have passed through my hands. I may be new here, but I am well aware of all the scandals you have committed. I have thoroughly researched your entire history. So, it will only take me a few seconds to put you in your place. Now answer the questions I ask. Where were you on the day when your brother, Kalu Singh, was killed?"

Lalu Singh: "My farmhouse, I went there. When I was in Jaisalmer, the land was taken, and then, for some reason, I went to Hanumangarh. After so many years, I came to Jaisalmer to sell this farmhouse. I also have the property papers of the farmhouse if you want to see them."

Jaspal: "Do you know that there was a murder of your own brother, Kalu Singh, within 2 kilometers of your farmhouse, and you were there at that time."

Lalu Singh: "Why would I kill my brother? We had some differences, but it's been 10 years."

Jaspal: "Hmm… Until this case is solved, you won't go anywhere from Jaisalmer. Understand?"

Lalu Singh: "Okay. You solve the case. I am here. And if my words or behavior have offended you, I apologize."

Jaspal: "If you had maintained this behavior from the beginning, you wouldn't have to apologize." (Folding hands) "Ghanni khamma."

Lalu Singh sits in the car and drives away.

Nathuram: "Sir, you should not have spoken to him in this way."

Jaspal: "Nathu, he is a criminal, and you want me to talk to him with respect."

Nathuram: "Sir, I'm just afraid that something wrong might happen now."

Location: Bhimnagar, Jaisalmer

Time: 3:00 (Afternoon)

Scene – Kaishav Jain converted a bungalow into a fake hospital, named Nayak Hospital. With this idea, Kaishav Jain's men, Khetu and Vikram, became fake doctors.

After a while, a jeep arrives, from which an elderly man and a woman get off.

According to the plan, pillows were placed on the bed in the fake ICU, and a sheet was placed on it to make it look like someone was lying on the bed. Khetu and Vikram show Reena's parents from outside the door of the ICU that Reena is still unconscious, and her condition is not right, but she will be fine in a few days.

Reena's parents say, "We will stay here until Reena is well."

Vikram: "Oh, you don't need to stay. The hotel owner will bear the entire cost of treatment. We will take care of everything, and when Reena gets well, we will call you. Anyway, there is no arrangement to stay here. And if you stay in a hotel, you will spend money unnecessarily. We are here; your daughter will return home safe and sound."

After giving a lot of assurance, Reena's parents expressed gratitude and left, reassured that their daughter was in good hands.

Location: Rasesar Colony, Jaisalmer

Time: 2:00 PM (Next day)

Jaspal is reading a newspaper at home, and Shantidevi is preparing food in the kitchen. Khushi is happily returning home from school on the bus. The bus stops in front of Jaspal's house. Khushi gets off the bus carrying her school bag and crutches. The bus then continues on its way. Khushi is slowly walking toward her house. Suddenly, a car from behind, speeding at a fast pace, hits Khushi, dragging her in front of another house and colliding with a car parked there. The collision triggers an alarm. The car that caused the accident backs up and ruthlessly runs over Khushi again before speeding away for the third time. The siren is blaring, and the entire neighborhood rushes out. Shanti Devi comes out and faints upon seeing her daughter's lifeless body. The limbs of the body are scattered in all directions. Jaspal rushes out, and what is visible are the scattered shreds of the body. Jaspal, in a state of shock, walks away. The sound of people screaming echoes in his ears, and tears fill his eyes. For the first time, Jaspal's hands and feet trembled; fear took over his entire body. The siren is still blaring, and the atmosphere is filled with horror. Beautiful eyes that used to be filled with laughter are now lying scattered on the road.

Present:

Place: Tihar Jail, Delhi

Time: 09:00 PM

Ramanuj: "Who was in the car?"

Bindu: "If you still haven't figured it out, then perhaps I have doubts about your degree."

Ramanuj: "As far as I heard, you have no faults. Then why are you in jail? What circumstances led you to this state?"

Bindu: "Fate had written my biography until now. But what will happen now is the most unfortunate period of my life. Not only me but no one will survive this destruction. This is just the beginning; destruction is yet to come."

There was a strange fear in his voice, as if the shadow of dark clouds was about to spread across all corners. In his eyes was hidden sorrow and the story of remorse. Listening to the tale of his life and self-reproach, Ramanuj felt the realization of the impending dreadful history. He knew that Bindu's next story would be as mysterious and terrifying as it could be, and hearing it would have a profound impact on his life.

Ramanuj: "I'll be there in 2 minutes."

Ramanuj proceeds to the bathroom, cleans his face, and advances toward the Bindu's cell. At that moment, his attention is drawn to the news displayed on the television.

[This is the hotel where thousands of innocents met their tragic end. Yes, this is 'The Titan Hotel.' Once, an era knew little about this grand and splendid hotel, and now, discussions about it are on every person's lips. Today, this hotel has metamorphosed into a tourist destination, attracting individuals from every corner of the globe who come to witness its haunting history. Every wall of the hotel stands as a testimony to the screams that once echoed within, bearing witness to the unimaginable horrors that unfolded during that dreadful period.]

Upon entering the confines of the Bindu Jail, Ramanuj states,

"Proceed with your story…"